a better me

ALY WELCH

WRITING BLOC

INDIE PUBLISHING TEAM

one

"BRI, where the hell are the extras?" The assistant director's harsh voice blared over Gabrielle Johnson's headset. She almost dropped the bag of bite-size candy bars and fruit chews she was pouring into a large plastic bowl in a break room set aside for craft service.

"Still in holding, sir." Gabrielle hoped Chase Davis did not notice the way she hesitated on the "sir."' Though he had spent most of the day taking his ineptitude out on production assistants like Gabrielle, his foul mood would only worsen if he detected any attitude in return. Her job was to put out proverbial fires, not start them. "Do you need me to bring them to set?"

"Nah, I just like to keep tabs on where they are." Somehow his snide, nasal voice sounded even more grating over her headset. If only she had let the battery pack for his headset die instead of racing to find him a replacement earlier. "Yeah, I need you to bring them! Just a couple of old guys that can play chess in the background of our next shot."

"Be right there."

Gabrielle left the break room. She strode down the hall into a larger room full of bored extras scrolling through their phones or talking in hushed tones. Most sat in cubicles like holding pens. The office had an open floor plan with those short partition walls that were meant to encourage teamwork—at least during the regular work week. A production company shooting a film in Buffalo had rented the downtown office building Friday night through the weekend.

Gabrielle cringed at the thought of working in such an office. Being confined to a more conventional cubicle held little appeal, but the relative peace and privacy of higher partition walls had to be preferable. She often reminded herself how little she desired a traditional nine-to-five career when subjected to arrogant crew members like Chase during tougher gigs. At least she only had to deal with him today. Tomorrow she would be driving home for spring break...although that meant dealing with her parents instead.

Out of the frying pan, into the fire.

Gabrielle sighed. She walked across the room to a couple of old men in bathrobes and pajamas. They'd been talking and nudging each other as they leered at some young women dressed in nursing scrubs across the room.

"Excuse me," she said. The men turned to leer at her instead. "We need you for the next shot. Follow me, please."

Gabrielle led the men to the elevator, sensing the weight of their stares on her back - or at least she hoped it was her back. Her ears burned.

"What's a pretty girl like you doing behind the scenes when you should be on camera?" Gabrielle could smell today's lunch on the old man's breath: bacon cheeseburgers with grilled onions. She turned away, suppressing a shudder as she pressed the button for the third floor, as he continued. "If you want, maybe I could put in a good word for you with the director for some screen time."

Gabrielle remembered Chase mentioning that this man owned the building they were filming in. His name was Mickey Mc...something-or-other. She turned to give him a quick smile. "No, but thank you." The elevator doors opened. "Right this way, please." Gabrielle

2

turned to lead the men to a room staged to look like the rec room of a nursing home.

Chase appeared in the doorway. "Where's the nurse?"

Startled, she met his watery brown eyes with a look of confusion. "But you never –

"Damn it, Bri!" The thirtysomething glared from under a Yankees baseball cap, which concealed a prematurely receding hairline. "We have to film two more scenes for B roll before we can wrap, or this shoot gets pushed out another day. I'll set these two. Get the nurse. Now."

"Aww. Be nice to the kid," Mickey McDeathBreath said. "She's been a real sweetheart to us." He squeezed Gabrielle's shoulder with his warm bony fingers.

Gabrielle stiffened but left without another word.

* * *

"You'd better get it together if you want more work going forward." Chase pushed past Gabrielle in a huff, causing her to drop a stack of paperwork.

Though it was an empty threat, his words still stung. Gabrielle did not bother to remind him that most of the day's failings were his own. Chase was struggling in the first gig he'd scored as an assistant director after relocating to New York City, and it was just a low budget independent film that brought him back to his hometown. Meanwhile, Gabrielle had already lined up work on a Hollywood production filming in western New York later this month. Some romantic comedy called *A New Man*. She doubted she would be subjected to Chase again any time soon.

"Nice to see you again, too," Gabrielle muttered. She knelt to pick up all the forms and time sheets she'd dropped. After she gave them to another crew member, Gabrielle grabbed her backpack and slung it over her shoulder. A few crew members nodded or waved as she walked by. She gave them a shaky smile on her way out the door.

. . .

"Are they always so handsy?"

Gabrielle turned from her car to look at the speaker, a pretty blonde she recognized as one of the nurses. Hailey or Bailey or something, a newcomer to the scene.

"The other extras, I mean?" The blonde tucked a strand of hair behind her ear.

Gabrielle frowned. "Did something happen?"

"That gross old man grabbed me while we were filming the scene in the rec room. I was supposed to refill their juice. Almost spilled it all over the place. I didn't say anything at the time because the cameras were rolling, and the director already seemed like he was in a bad mood, ya know?"

"Was it the old man in the green bathrobe?"

Hailey-or-Bailey nodded.

"Ick. He owns this building. He's not one of the regulars. If any of them behaved like that, none of the local agencies would ask them back." Gabrielle gave her a reassuring smile.

"So, it's not, like, a typical thing?"

Gabrielle's smile faltered. "Every film is a different adventure. Stuff like that definitely doesn't happen a lot, though, no. If anything like that happens again, let a PA know right away so we can take care of it."

Hailey-or-Bailey looked doubtful.

"If we work together again, I'll make sure you aren't around anyone sketchy." Gabrielle offered another reassuring smile as she opened her car door. "Try to enjoy the rest of your evening."

* * *

"Rough day at the office?"

Gabrielle collapsed beside her dark-haired roommate Sean on a black futon mattress atop a pale wooden frame. The futon was a robust example of Swedish engineering they'd built together the previous year for their first big test as roommates. She rested her head on his shoulder and sighed. "Aren't they all?"

"So dramatic. Are you sure you don't want to be an actress?"

"Ugh. Definitely not." Gabrielle sat up straight and filled Sean in on her day, including her encounters with the handsy old guy and the unfortunate extra. "You know, it's usually not as bad as outsiders like my parents think, but it isn't always some big shot Hollywood producer, either. I think I've encountered a random creeper at every level of production. Even in catering." She wrinkled her nose in disgust.

"Creepers are everywhere," Sean agreed. "Oh, God. Do you remember your old manager at Bert's Bar and Grill?"

"Yuck." Gabrielle scooted away from Sean. "I try not to."

"I bet Chase has seen some shit now that he lives in New York City. I heard a rumor he's mostly bartending and working temp jobs to pay the rent. This was his first big movie gig."

"It showed." Gabrielle hugged a throw pillow to her chest, flipping the sequins on the front from black to vibrant shades of blue and green. "Honestly, I'm not sure I want to do this much longer. It's not like I'm going to work my way up any higher. Maybe I should just get some boring old office job after I get my degree. At least then I'd have benefits and a steady paycheck. It would make my parents happy."

"You would've done a better job than Chase today, and you know it," Sean said. "Knowing him, you probably saved his ass. Wouldn't be the first time. You just need to be more assertive."

"Yeah, sure, because that never backfires." Gabrielle sighed.

Sean rolled his eyes. He stood up and smoothed his pants. Only then did Gabrielle realize he was dressed for a night out, his thick hair fashionably tousled and his green eyes lined and shadowed with something shimmery.

"Are you going out?"

"Meeting friends at the club." Sean grinned. "And before you ask, no. Monica won't be there. I think she's seeing a waiter in the South-towns now."

"The one she—"

Sean waved away Gabrielle's question. "Nah, different guy. C'mere, give me a hug before I go."

Gabrielle rose from the couch. She threw her arms around Sean and pressed her head into his. He pulled away to give her a quick kiss on the cheek before he took his jacket off the hook beside the door. "Text me when you get to your parents' house tomorrow, okay?"

"I wanna stay with you."

Sean laughed. "Just relax. Enjoy your break."

"Have you met my parents?" Gabrielle pulled away to look up at him. "They're not so good for the relaxing."

"Keep a low profile and catch up with old friends, then." Sean grabbed a set of keys beside the door. He looked back at Gabrielle with an encouraging smile. "I'll see you when you get back."

Old friends.

Gabrielle released a mirthless chuckle at the thought of these nonexistent friends the following morning. She pulled her used blue Honda Civic into the driveway of her parents' home in a quiet suburb of Syracuse. She saw that her parents had replaced the faded red exterior shutters on their white two-story home with yellow ones. The lawn had been mowed, and the first blooms of the season—tulips—painted the garden red, orange, and yellow. She'd grown up in this house, but it felt so foreign and strange every time she returned to it now.

Her mother, a slender woman with glossy brown hair and blue eyes, opened the door before Gabrielle could even knock. She was still dressed for work in a tailored navy blazer over a silky cream shirt and a matching navy pencil skirt.

"Honestly." Mrs. Johnson ushered Gabrielle into the house and dug in before the front door even clicked shut. "I don't know why you had to go to a university clear across the state when there are excellent schools within a few minutes' drive, but even the Finger Lakes would have been better. I bet you could have gotten into Cornell had you studied more for your SATs. Bigger movies come through here, too, but I don't know why you couldn't have picked a more practical industry to work in."

"Honey, at least wait until she's settled into her room before you start lecturing the poor kid." Her father, whose dark hair was graying at the temples, barely glanced up from his book as Gabrielle dropped her duffle bag on the floor. "How was the drive?"

"Fine, thanks." Gabrielle turned to face her mother. "I'm a junior, Mom. Thought you'd be over it by now."

"You don't have to be a smart a...aleck. Now go put your bag in your room and freshen up. I made a reservation for dinner." Mrs. Johnson turned to her husband with a knowing smile.

Mr. Johnson looked at Gabrielle for the first time since she arrived, lowering his reading glasses. "For the record, I had nothing to do with this. Don't blame me for whatever happens next." Gabrielle raised an eyebrow, but her father would say no more. Instead, he adjusted his glasses and went back to reading.

"I hope you brought something nicer to wear." Mrs. Johnson looked at Gabrielle's baggy hoodie and rumpled jeans with a look of distaste. "And see if you can do something with that hair of yours."

Gabrielle stared at herself in the bathroom mirror. Her face appeared paler than usual under the bronzer her mother insisted upon applying. She winced as Mrs. Johnson twisted her auburn hair into a chignon at the nape of her neck, securing it with coppery bobby pins. The bathroom was pristine (or at least it had been until strands of Gabrielle's hair littered the white porcelain sink) with pale blue green walls and stone tiles on the floor.

"Maybe if I curl some of these loose strands." Mrs. Johnson pursed her lips as she regarded a few strands of stray hairs with a critical eye. "All these split ends. Maybe I shouldn't use an iron after all." She let go of Gabrielle's hair, shaking her head.

"I don't understand why you're making such a big deal about dinner. I just drove for several hours. In holiday weekend traffic, which was an absolute nightmare. I'm tired." Gabrielle yawned to punctuate the point. "I wanted to relax tonight."

Mrs. Johnson glared at Gabrielle's reflection. "You can relax tomorrow. Tonight, we're catching up with some old friends downtown."

"If they're old friends, then they already know what I look like." Gabrielle's eyes narrowed with distrust as she noted her mother's elegant black sheath dress. . Mrs. Johnson even had pearls fastened around her neck—the strand her mother-in-law gave her that she only wore for family occasions. But Gabrielle knew Grandpa and Grandma Johnson were vacationing in the Florida Keys, so they couldn't be the dinner guests. "Why all the extra effort?"

Mrs. Johnson ignored Gabrielle's question. "I laid out a new dress I bought for you on your bed, and a cardigan if you get cold. It's one of mine, but you can keep it if you like. I don't suppose you brought any dress shoes with you?"

Gabrielle shook her head, and a few more strands of hair fell from her chignon.

Mrs. Johnson sighed. "Good thing we wear the same size. I'll loan you a pair of my shoes. Try not to scuff them."

Gabrielle shrugged. "I could just wear my sneakers."

Mrs. Johnson glared. "You are not wearing sneakers with a dress."

Gabrielle opened her mouth to protest.

"You are *wearing* the dress. It's a nice restaurant, not one of those awful dives you used to work at." Mrs. Johnson frowned. "You're not still waitressing, are you?"

"No, but I've considered dancing as a side hustle." Gabrielle struck an exaggerated pose and made a duck face at her reflection.

"Lovely."

Mrs. Johnson's frown deepened as she gazed at Gabrielle in the mirror. After a moment, she turned to go, her heels clicking against the hardwood floor as she strode down the hall into the master bedroom. Gabrielle reached for a tissue to wipe away some of the makeup until she looked more like herself. It was going to be a long spring break.

"The other party is already here."

The hostess led Gabrielle and her parents to a large round booth in a dark corner of the upscale steakhouse. When the occupants looked up, Gabrielle's heart sank. She turned to glare at her parents. Keeping his hand low, Mr. Johnson pointed a thumb in his wife's direction.

Mrs. Johnson ignored her husband and daughter. She gave the trio at the table a broad, if strained, smile as she slid into the booth across from them. "Jim, Stacy, it's so good to see you again."

Jim Williams shook their hands before sitting down beside his wife. Jim was tall. He had gray hair with a receding hairline, and the broad shoulders and pot belly of a former athlete whose best days were long behind him. Stacy, a diminutive blonde with hazel eyes, mirrored Mrs. Johnson's tight smile, but Gabrielle suspected Stacy owed hers to one too many Botox treatments rather than mere discomfort.

"Gabrielle, you remember Brandon, don't you?" Mrs. Johnson turned to her with a pointed look.

Gabrielle slid into the booth across from her former classmate. She muttered a half-hearted hello, fiddling with the top button of the cream-colored cardigan she wore over a floral dress as she looked down at the tablecloth.

"Hey, Gabby."

Though she cringed at the sound of her old nickname, Brandon used to call her worse when she had been unfortunate enough to land on his radar back in high school. She gazed at him from under her lowered eyelashes. He leaned back in the booth, dressed in an unbuttoned blue dress shirt over a white tee shirt, but something about his posture suggested defeat rather than the detached arrogance Gabrielle remembered. His brown eyes were distant; his dirty blond hair appeared almost disheveled, and not in the fashionable way her roommate Sean styled his own hair. There were faint shadows under his eyes.

"You'll have to excuse my son. It's been a rough couple of weeks since the accident. But Brandon is very happy to be here tonight, aren't you, Brandon?"

Brandon straightened in the booth, but his eyes remained distant.

"Accident?"

A waitress came to the table to take their drink orders before the Williamses could address Gabrielle's question. Gabrielle saw a glimmer of the old Brandon as he perked up at the sight of the waitress. Her dark brown hair was shiny and lustrous, not a split end to be seen.

"Brandon was in a car accident a few weeks ago," Mr. Williams clarified after they ordered drinks. Gabrielle noticed both he and Brandon stared as the slender but curvaceous waitress shimmied away in a black form-fitting skirt. Her father had his nose in the menu, and her mother glanced at Mrs. Williams with a look of sympathy.

"His ankle was crushed," Mrs. Williams continued, ignoring Mrs. Johnson's concerned gaze. "Brandon was in the running to be quarterback next fall, too."

"He still can be." Mr. Williams looked sternly at his son. "A few more weeks of physical therapy, and he should be good as new. Better, even." Brandon shifted uncomfortably in his seat as his father spoke.

"Don't put too much pressure on him. He's been through a lot," Mrs. Williams said.

Mrs. Johnson nudged Mr. Johnson, and he cleared his throat.

"I've heard you're majoring in broadcast and digital journalism," he said to Brandon. "How are you enjoying the program?"

Brandon relaxed, grinning. "I'm not really into the research or the writing side of things behind the scenes," he explained. "I'm most interested in being on camera. My original plan was to play for the NFL for a while, move into sports reporting, and work my way up to anchor."

"And what's your new plan?" Mr. Williams asked, his tone darkening as he glowered at his son.

The waitress returned with their drinks before Brandon could answer. After everyone placed their orders, Mrs. Johnson changed the subject. Now Gabrielle found herself under scrutiny.

"Brandon, I've heard the film department at your university is exceptional." Mrs. Johnson regarded her daughter with a sidelong glance. "I was hoping Gabrielle would consider transferring to finish out her last year closer to home. I think there's a lot more opportunities for work here, too."

Brandon gave a noncommittal shrug. "I guess so. Like I said, I'm into broadcasting. We share studio space with the film department, but I don't know all that much about it."

"Well, maybe you could give Gabrielle a tour of the campus while she's home for spring break."

"Maybe..." Brandon's tone suggested he would rather continue discussing his future plans with his father.

"You don't have to do that." Gabrielle turned to glare at her mother. "I'm not transferring schools my last year. Besides, I've made all sorts of connections and things in Buffalo. Oh, and Rochester, too. That's important in this business."

"And you'd still have those connections," Mrs. Johnson said. "This way you could make even more connections. Is there any reason why you have to limit yourself to one region?" She continued before Gabrielle could answer. "Not only would you be able to find steady work, you could probably be more selective. Focus on the bigger projects."

"Your mother does have a point."

Gabrielle's jaw dropped as she looked at her father, betrayed.

Brandon chuckled. "Hey, I'm just glad I'm not the only one," he said as his parents glared at him. "I think that's ours." He looked away from them as servers approached the table.

The conversation moved away from schools and careers while everyone ate. Gabrielle consumed her steak and fries eagerly, evading most of the discussion, but every now and then she sensed Brandon's eyes on her. She pretended not to notice as she took another sip of her soda. Gabrielle sputtered and reached for her napkin to cover her face as some of the soda went up her nose.

Brandon laughed even more loudly than before. "Some things never change."

Gabrielle glared at him over her napkin.

Dinner could not end soon enough.

* * *

"Apart from the food, especially that steak – wow! - that was the exact opposite of an enjoyable evening." Mr. Johnson unlocked the car with his key fob. "We should definitely not do it again sometime."

Mrs. Johnson sighed, but she did not argue as he held the door open for her to sit down on the passenger side.

"I'm just glad this whole thing was about school, and Mom wasn't trying to set me up with that creep." Gabrielle climbed into the backseat, folding her arms across her chest and leaning back after buckling her seatbelt.

"Right." Mr. Johnson avoided meeting her eyes in the rearview mirror. "Still, it wouldn't hurt to humor your mother. Maybe one of us should take you around the campus instead of Brandon."

Gabrielle did not answer. Instead, she stared out the window as her father drove them home. Her reflection stared back, looking even wearier than before.

two

"HAVE you ever heard of Simone Weaver?"

Gabrielle groaned and burrowed deeper under her pillows. "Have you ever heard of sleeping in on vacation?"

"It's almost noon." Mrs. Johnson opened the blinds. "Were you on your phone all night?"

Gabrielle forced herself to sit up, squinting as harsh daylight poured into the room. "Yeah, I slipped Brandon my number when you weren't looking." She yawned, rubbing her eyes. "I sent him the link to my cam girl account. Then we spent the whole night sexting."

Mrs. Johnson's eyes widened for a moment before her face settled into a bemused glare, her lips pursed. "Simone Weaver is a life coach. She's written all sorts of books. She even has her own YouTube channel. She's doing a book signing at the mall today. I thought we'd go. Make a day of it, just the two of us."

Her mother dropped a paperback book on the bed. Gabrielle picked it up. A blond woman in a bright pink blazer beamed up at her against a pale blue background under the darker blue title, *A Better You*. She turned it over. "A young woman's guide to successfully navigating the business world with spunk and confidence," read the back.

"A self-help book? Seriously?"

"Oh, now, don't look at me like that. She's very engaging and has a lot of practical tips you can even apply in your line of work, such as it is. Check out a few chapters before we go so you and Ms. Weaver have something to talk about." Mrs. Johnson turned to leave but stopped and looked back at Gabrielle. "You...you don't really have a cam girl account, do you?"

Gabrielle merely shrugged with a quick lift of her eyebrows, then pressed her lips together in a demure grin. She opened the book to feign interest in reading.

Mrs. Johnson left the room with another one of her heavy sighs.

Gabrielle waited beside her mother outside the bookstore. She refrained from leaning her head against the glass as her gaze briefly flitted to the tired eyes of her reflection. Gabrielle tucked a loose strand of hair behind her ear and turned to face the courtyard at the mall. She inhaled sharply as a pretty platinum blonde in a vibrant purple off-shoulder sweater and tight denim miniskirt strode up to her.

"Gabby, is that you?"

"Hi, Emma." Gabrielle forced a smile. "How are you?"

"Oh my gosh, I'm *so* good. I started interning at Daddy's law office. And get this!" Her hazel eyes flashed with excitement as she lifted her hand. "I'm engaged!"

"Wow, it's...wow." Gabrielle stared at the large sparkling diamond surrounded by pink gems and set in an ornate platinum band. She wondered how Emma managed to support its substantial weight on her slender ring finger.

"Congratulations." Mrs. Johnson beamed at Emma.

"Thank you. So, what have you been up to?" Emma glanced at the book in Gabrielle's hands.

Gabrielle lowered it to her side, her hand and wrist obscuring the title on the front cover. "Mostly school," she said. "But I get a lot of PA work, too..."

"Personal assistant?" Emma arched a perfectly shaped eyebrow as she took in Gabrielle's disheveled appearance.

"Production assistant. You know, like, movies?"

"Oh, so you're the one who sorts the candies by color for the actors." Emma laughed. "I've heard that's a thing. Nobody wants those orange and yellow candies." Mrs. Johnson laughed, and Emma turned back to Gabrielle. "So, Miss Hollywood, have you run into anyone interesting?"

"Not lately." Gabrielle bit her lip on a smirk.

"Oh." Emma tilted her head as she considered Gabrielle's mild expression. She forced another bright smile, then said, "Well, gotta go. Bye, Gabby!" Emma darted off.

"I didn't know you two were friends."

Gabrielle turned to regard her mother; her expression pained. "I'm not sure I'd call Emma a friend," she said. As was the case with Brandon, Gabrielle had rarely been on Hailey's radar in high school, and that was how she preferred it. "She's probably just showing her ring to anyone who stands still long enough."

"You're a late bloomer. You've still got plenty of time to meet someone." Mrs. Johnson squeezed Gabrielle's arm. "I'd rather you focus on establishing your career anyway."

"Wait, what?" Gabrielle gaped at her mother, aghast. "That's not why I said...you didn't even marry Dad until you were almost thir-"

The line moved forward before Gabrielle finished her sentence. She found herself standing in front of the beaming face of Simone Weaver, which was framed by a sleek blond chin-length bob. The life coach had to be close to Gabrielle's mother in age, but the corners of her blue eyes barely crinkled when she smiled, and her forehead was smooth. She did not have that strange tight look Brandon's mother had, though.

Better plastic surgeon, Gabrielle supposed.

"And what's your name?" Simone took the book from Gabrielle's outstretched hand.

"Gabrielle."

"We just loved your book," Mrs. Johnson interjected. "My daughter chose the film industry over a more stable career like her father and I have - we're both in accounting - but I feel like a lot of your tips are still applicable. I think I remember reading you'd be in town for a week doing private consultations. Do you still have appointments available?"

Simone's glazed eyes lowered to Mrs. Johnson's designer handbag at the end of her speech, lighting up. "The film industry, did you say?" She turned to Gabrielle. "Actress?"

"Oh God, no," Gabrielle said. "I'm working as a production assistant for the moment."

Simone's lips curved down into a faint frown as she considered.

"But I might want to work my way up the ladder someday!" Gabrielle added when her mother nudged her side. Then she winced, realizing she might have cost herself an easy way out.

Simone's face broadened into a grin. "In that case, I think you'd certainly want to improve your business acumen." She wrote something in the book, then reached for a business card and jotted a number on the back. "I'm staying at the Hilton downtown. Contact me later, and I'll see if I can fit you in."

"Thank you so much." Once the ink dried, Mrs. Johnson accepted the book and business card and slipped them into her purse.

* * *

Mrs. Johnson spent the rest of the afternoon dragging Gabrielle from store to store to buy an assortment of suits, blouses, slim-fitting jeans, and even another dress: a body-hugging sheath with wide straps in navy. "You may not have a corporate position, but you're still a professional. Your wardrobe should reflect that."

Gabrielle did not bother saying that even most big-name directors favored jeans and ball caps over suits and ties. She knew her mother would not be swayed. Instead, she allowed herself to be swept through the mall, offering her halfhearted approval or disapproval to the myriad of clothes her mother made her try on. Only when Gabrielle's stomach rumbled did Mrs. Johnson relent to lunch.

"You're an adult now," Mrs. Johnson began as they settled into the booth of a Mexican restaurant.

Gabrielle raised an eyebrow. So good of her mother to notice.

"You can order a drink if you'd like. No need to put on airs around your father and I. Oh, don't look at me like that. I remember what college is like. Just so long as you're careful. I remember how awful frat boys can be, too. Not to mention all of those Hollywood types you hang out with."

Gabrielle kept her lack of interaction with frat boys *or* Hollywood types to herself. Let her mother think she was a social butterfly flitting from one party to another; it was one less thing to be lectured about, the importance of networking and schmoozing and all that contrived bullshit she knew to be her biggest weakness. Instead, she told her mother, "Soda's fine."

"Well, I'm getting a margarita." Mrs. Johnson removed her tailored suede jacket and folded it neatly beside her in the booth before setting her purse on top.

A waitress came to take their orders. Gabrielle dipped a tortilla chip into a bowl of queso after the waitress returned with drinks and an appetizer. . She reached for another chip but stopped when she saw her mother looking at her with a furrowed brow.

"Are you happy, Bri?"

Gabrielle blinked, taken aback. "I'm not *not* happy."

Mrs. Johnson shook her head. "And there it is. You're always so evasive and noncommittal. It's impossible to get a straight answer from you about anything. You just don't seem to be as invested in yourself and your future as you should be. It worries me."

"I...I guess I prefer to live in the moment."

And in that moment, Gabrielle wanted to eat her chips and queso in peace.

"Are you, though?" Mrs. Johnson pressed. "Living, I mean."

Gabrielle shrugged. "I'm not *not* living."

Mrs. Johnson sighed, taking a sip from her margarita as she watched Gabrielle eat in silence.

* * *

Later, Gabrielle sat on her bed with her phone in one hand and Simone Weaver's business card in the other. She wondered if the self-help author expected a phone call or if she could text her instead. Gabrielle decided to text. If it was the wrong move, maybe Simone Weaver would blow her off, letting her off the hook.

Hi, this is Bri Johnson. We spoke at your book signing. My mother wanted me to schedule a meeting with you. Thanks.

To her immense disappointment, Gabrielle received a curt reply a few minutes later.

Hi. Can see you tomorrow at 3. Room 315.

Her hotel room?

Gabrielle shrugged. Simone Weaver was just an author, not some sketchy Hollywood bigwig. She decided she felt relieved to get the meeting over with so she could have the rest of spring break to relax.

The next day, Gabrielle humored her mother by wearing a new pair of jeans and a crisp white button-down blouse. She ran a hand through her unruly auburn curls as she walked out to her car. With a pang of sadness, she noticed a hint of rust on the frame of her otherwise vivid blue Honda Civic, an unfortunate consequence of the salt they used to melt the ice and snow in the winter.

"You should really take some notes." Mrs. Johnson followed her, proffering a notebook and fountain pen.

Gabrielle took them, wincing as her mother kissed her cheek.

"You know I love you, right?"

Gabrielle nodded. "Love you, too." She opened the car door and sat.

"Be safe," her mother added.

"Always."

Gabrielle gave her mother a quick smile before turning the key in the ignition and backing out of the driveway.

three

GABRIELLE FELT uneasy as she handed her car keys to the valet at the hotel. The feeling lingered as she approached the front desk. "Um, I have a three o'clock appointment with Simone Weaver in room 315?"

"Name?"

"Bri Johnson."

The woman uncapped a bright pink highlighter as she referred to a list of names and times in a binder. She crossed off Gabrielle's name. "You can go on up, Miss Johnson."

Gabrielle approached the elevators. Two older gentlemen in golf attire walked into one, so she waited for the next to descend in hopes of being alone with her thoughts. Gabrielle wondered if she should have prepared questions for Simone Weaver in advance, but she realized she had no idea what she would even ask. She could only hope the meeting would go quickly and painlessly.

A young man and woman, whom Gabrielle presumed to be newlyweds, ran into the elevator just before the doors closed, giggling and groping one another like they were the last two people in the world. Gabrielle clutched the notebook and pencil to her chest, trying to ignore the sound of their eager kissing. She considered clearing her throat but decided against it.

Gabrielle felt a momentary sense of relief as she stepped out of the elevator at the third floor. She contemplated how many floors the newlyweds had left and whether they'd make it with their fancy attire intact, wrinkling her nose at the intrusive image as she walked down the hall.

Her earlier trepidation returned when she reached room 315 and knocked on the heavy wooden door.

Simone Weaver opened the door with a welcoming smile, smelling of a soft but heady perfume. "Bri, come in," she said, as if they were old friends.

Simone wore a cream oversized designer sweater, black leggings, and ballet flats, looking magazine perfect. She guided Gabrielle to a pair of opulent chairs with pink, green, and gold damask cushions and ornately carved wooden legs. They were located beside a picture window that overlooked the city. "I just made the most amazing lavender chamomile tea. Would you like some?"

"Yes, please."

Gabrielle sat in one of the chairs. She opened the notebook and sat poised with her pencil.

"Oh, we don't need to be as formal as all that."

Simone set down two porcelain cups with gold trim on the small wooden table between the chairs. She plucked the notebook and pencil from Gabrielle's fingers to set them beside the teacups on the table. Simone handed one cup to Gabrielle, then reached for her own as she sat across from her in the other chair.

"So, Bri, tell me about yourself."

Simone leaned forward, watching Gabrielle with genuine interest as she took a sip of tea.

"Um, I don't really know what to tell you. My name is Gabrielle, but I prefer Bri. I'm a junior in college. I'm going for a degree in film. I also work part-time as a production assistant."

"That's what you do," Simone said, setting her cup of tea down on the table. "But it doesn't tell me who you *are*. Your hopes and dreams." Simone leaned further forward, her lips curving into a sly smile. "What makes Bri Johnson tingle?"

Gabrielle furrowed her brow.

"Oh, relax. Not like that." Simone chuckled as she leaned back in her chair, reaching for her tea once more. "I could have asked what makes you tick, but I hate that word. It's so mechanical. Inhuman. You're a person, not a clock."

"Oh. Um, I'm not really sure." Gabrielle took a sip of her own tea. The floral notes confused her taste buds, but there was something comforting yet mysterious and tantalizing about the flavor. She took another sip as she considered Simone's question.

"'Don't really know', 'not really sure'." Simone regarded Gabrielle with a stern look. "I'm sorry to be harsh with you, Bri, but you're not going to get very far in this world if you're always so unsure of yourself." Her expression softened back into a smile. "Sometimes it's a lot more important to convey confidence in your knowledge and abilities than to actually have it."

Gabrielle tilted her head. "Confidence? Or knowledge and abilities?"

Simone threw her head back as she laughed. "Any of the above."

Gabrielle thought of Chase. "I guess that's true."

"You guess?"

Gabrielle gave a rueful grin. "It's true. It's definitely true." She continued drinking her tea, enjoying the warmth as it spread from her stomach all the way into the tips of her fingers.

"Look at that. A genuine smile." Simone's own grin widened. "So much of getting ahead in this world is finding the right balance of authenticity and performance. Something tells me people never look past your insecurities to see the real you. Let me help you with that." Her skin took on a strange bluish sheen.

Gabrielle blinked.

The bluish sheen was gone.

Gabrielle took another sip.

"What are your goals? Do you want to pursue a career in film?"

Gabrielle nodded slowly, feeling lightheaded. She wondered if she'd had enough to eat for breakfast. Gabrielle forced herself to focus on Simone's unlined face and ignore the way the air seemed to churn and shimmer around the woman's silhouette like heat rising from hot pavement in the summer sun. The bluish sheen had returned to her strange, ageless skin.

"But not acting?"

Gabrielle giggled. "Definitely not. I want to direct. Wow. I've never said that out loud before." Her hands were starting to tremble, but she took another sip of tea before she set her cup on the table.

She missed.

Aghast, Gabrielle stared as the cup fell, shattering and spilling tea on the hardwood floor.

"Oh, don't worry your pretty little head about it." Simone knelt to gather up the pieces of broken porcelain in her hand. As Simone stood back up, Gabrielle found herself staring into her own smirking reflection.

It winked at her.

And Gabrielle's world went dark.

four

SITTING on the unmade bed in his studio apartment, Brandon stared down at Gabby Johnson's number on his phone. His weekend had not gone well, not after his father received a phone call from Brandon's physician regarding insurance. He should have read those stupid forms more carefully before giving permission for his parents to receive medical information. Now his father knew that toxicology reports following the accident had uncovered steroids in his system. It was not the sort of thing that resulted in a DUI charge, but it did not bode well for his future in football.

Oh well.

He wouldn't have been able to hide the truth from his parents forever, not when the university's football department was set to rule on his continued involvement in the program. Besides, his accident had made the local news. It would only be a matter of time before some nosy reporter uncovered the dirt on him. Maybe that girl from his school's journalism department he'd gone out with the other month, the pretty brunette who interned with the local paper. She seemed like the sort of girl who would hold a grudge.

How many angry texts had she sent?

Maybe Brandon shouldn't have been so quick to blow her off.

Now he was considering slumming it with some nerd he went to high school with after he failed to score the number of that hot waitress.

Brandon ran a hand through his already messy hair. He typed a message offering to show Gabrielle the campus and hit send. He set the phone down on the bed and laid back with his hands laced behind his head. Brandon felt unsurprised when he heard a beep soon after. He sat up, reaching for the phone to read her reply.

I can think of better ways to spend the afternoon.

Brandon raised an eyebrow, a smile tugging at the corner of his lips. He thought for a moment, then replied:

What did you have in mind?

Tell me when and where, and I'll let you know when I get there.

Quite the difference from her reserved demeanor at dinner last night. Then again, the lack of parental guidance might account for the saucier behavior. Still, Gabby Johnson was a strange one. She was not as curvy as his usual type, but her face was pretty enough. And he'd always heard gingers could be wild. If nothing else, maybe she'd take his mind off his problems for a few hours. Brandon replied with his address and suggested one o'clock. Then he muted his phone and crawled under his rumpled sheets to go to sleep.

"You look pretty today."

Gabrielle looked at her mother in surprise.

"My meetings are done for the day, so I'm working from home the rest of the afternoon." Mrs. Johnson still wore a suit, but she traded her heels for a pair of flats in the entry. "Are you going out?"

"Um, yeah." Gabrielle tucked a strand of auburn hair behind her ear as she followed Mrs. Johnson into the home office and leaned against the doorway. "Brandon offered to show me around campus today."

"Oh, I didn't know he reached out to you. I hope you don't mind that I gave him your number. Your father didn't seem to like him much, though I suppose that's his paternal duty. Besides, it's not like it's a date or anything." Mrs. Johnson sat at the table, opening her laptop. "I think that top you're wearing is my favorite."

Gabrielle played with the collar of the silky jewel blue shirt she'd paired with dark denim jeans. "Yeah, it's alright, I guess." She ran a hand through her hair, frowning at how quickly she reached the ends.

"I'm not sure if I'd go with those dress shoes, though. You'll get blisters. Better switch to sneakers. The new ones, not those beat-up things you came home from school in."

Gabrielle glanced down at her heels. "Oh. Right."

"And, honey?"

"Yeah...?

"Be safe."

"Okay, Mom. Bee."

Mrs. Johnson looked up, arching an eyebrow as she watched as the front door closed behind her daughter. "She forgot to change her shoes." Her gaze returned to the computer screen as she began to click through all of her emails from work. "A campus trek is one way to break them in, I suppose."

Brandon stepped out of the shower, wrapping a towel around his waist. He heard a knock on the front door of his studio apartment. Surprised, he checked the time on his smartphone. 2:12 PM. He must have dozed off in the shower.

"Just a minute."

Brandon considered dressing, but he wanted to find out how Gabrielle would react to the sight of him wearing only a towel. Maybe she'd turn and run, but it might be worth it just to see the look on her face. Or maybe she'd be down. Even better.

He strode across the room to the front door. Through the peephole, he saw Gabby's lean figure. She wore a silky blue shirt, unbuttoned low enough to offer a glimpse of her cleavage. Her curves appeared more generous today than they had in her mousier attire at the steakhouse.

Pleased, Brandon opened the door.

Gabrielle's eyes widened with surprise, but also appreciation, as she took in the sight of his muscular torso and legs. Her lips curved into a grin as she slipped past him into his apartment, smelling of vanilla and something spicier.

"You didn't have to get dressed up just for me."

Brandon closed the door with a rueful laugh. "I didn't notice the time." He turned to Gabrielle. At the restaurant, she'd seemed as shy and reserved as he remembered. Now, something about the way her eyes slid over his body made Brandon feel exposed. At least she seemed to like what she saw as she took a step toward him. She looked more like the Gabby he remembered as she gazed up at him from under heavy lashes, her blue eyes even more ravenous than they had been at the steakhouse when the servers brought her meal.

"So now what?"

Gabrielle's grin widened as she fiddled with a button on her blouse. Eager to regain control over the situation, Brandon lifted her chin with his index finger and leaned down to kiss her. Gabrielle pressed her hands against his chest as they kissed, then lowered them to his towel as she deepened the kiss.

"Still a little overdressed for my taste," she murmured against his lips as Brandon struggled to catch his breath. Gabby tugged the towel away, kissing him harder.

So much for regaining control.

Gabrielle awoke to late afternoon sunlight streaming in through the blinds of...

...was she in a hotel room?

Gabrielle tried to push herself up, but a muscular arm was draped across her body. Her naked body, she now realized, covered only by a thin sheet. A glance to her left revealed the arm belonged to none other than Brandon Williams. He stirred as she squirmed free of his grasp. Her eyes scanned the hotel room. She spotted her panties on the floor and her bra strewn haphazardly over a chair.

Then she was standing in front of the window, buttoning her shirt as she gazed at the road below, noting the lack of traffic. Brandon was standing behind her before she made sense of the lost time between rising from the bed and beginning to dress herself. She tried to shrug him off as he pushed aside her hair to nibble at her neck. With his free hand, he worked against her efforts to button her shirt.

"Stop that."

Gabrielle pushed aside his hand and moved away from him. Brandon pouted at her.

"What are we doing here?"

"Isn't it obvious?"

A smirk replaced Brandon's pout. Gabrielle sensed his nudity but kept her eyes on his face as she tried to piece together the events that brought them to this moment. She remembered walking down the hall to a hotel room. A woman had opened the door.

No.

Gabrielle walked down the hall, fully clothed.

It wasn't a memory.

It was now.

Brandon opened the door, pulling her into his arms.

A teacup fell to the floor.

It shattered.

Gabrielle stood in front of the window as the sun set over a quiet city skyline. Brandon stood behind her, kissing her neck as he unbuttoned her shirt.

A teacup fell to the floor.

five

MR. JOHNSON LOOKED up from his plate as the front door opened and Gabrielle walked inside. He sat with Mrs. Johnson at a table in the dining room across from the foyer, the remnants of a rice and chicken dish on his plate. "Windy downtown?"

"Huh?" Gabrielle cocked her head as she stared at him, confused. Then she reached up a hand to run through her tousled hair, tucking a strand behind one ear. "Oh, yeah. Totally."

"I tried calling to see if you'd be home in time for dinner, but you never answered your phone." Mrs. Johnson set down her fork and looked at Gabrielle, pursing her lips.

"Yeah, sorry. I ate."

Gabrielle walked into the dining room.

"How was the tour? Did you enjoy seeing the campus?"

"It was alright, I guess."

Mrs. Johnson chuckled at Gabrielle's noncommittal tone. "Well, thank you for humoring me. Will you be spending time with Brandon again before you go back to school?"

"The one we toured?" Gabrielle tilted her head to the side.

"No, in Buffalo." Mrs. Johnson shook her head, bemused. "Honestly, Gabrielle. How much time did you spend in the sun today? You seem a little out of it."

"Well, I mean, we walked around campus. Like, a lot."

"Where did you eat?"

"Uhm." Gabrielle pressed her lips together as she thought. "This French place downtown. Le Bistro Magnifique? They have this really amazing turkey sandwich with a cranberry aio...mayo. And rosemary parmesan frites. I mean, fries."

"Huh." Mrs. Johnson looked impressed. "And how was the company?"

Gabrielle smirked. "Not as good as that sandwich," she replied truthfully. "I'm kind of beat, though."

Mr. Johnson watched Gabrielle, but he drank his coffee and remained silent as his wife continued to speak.

"Yes, your feet must be killing you after all that walking."

"Totally."

Gabrielle gave a little shrug as she crossed the dining room to the hall. She paused, then entered the room on the right, closing the door behind her.

Mrs. Johnson turned to her husband. "You don't think...?"

"I try not to, no."

Mrs. Johnson walked into Gabrielle's room later that week. Gabrielle sat on the bed, eyes scanning her phone. "Staying in tonight?"

Gabrielle looked up and shrugged. "I dunno yet. Maybe."

Mrs. Johnson sat on the window seat by Gabrielle's bed. "What have you been up to these past few nights?" She gazed around the room, the bed with its rumpled aqua sheets and fluffy blanket, the walls adorned with posters of singers and bands she was not even sure Gabrielle listened to anymore. Then she looked at Gabrielle, who looked far too grown-up for her surroundings. "I know you haven't been with Brandon. He called me asking about you. Seemed a little anxious."

Even a little desperate, Mrs. Johnson thought, but kept the observation to herself.

"Yeah, he keeps trying to reach me. So I muted him."

"Did something happen? With Brandon?"

Now Gabrielle looked at her mother, lips pursed. "Nothing worth mentioning. He's just..." She paused, as though searching for the right word. "Brutish. I don't like that."

"No, I don't suppose you would." Mrs. Johnson stared down at the floor. "I'm sorry I gave him your number. I don't know what I was thinking."

"When should I head back, do you think?"

Mrs. Johnson looked up in confusion.

"To school," Gabrielle clarified. "I think I'm needed at work on Monday, too, but they haven't sent an official call time yet." She frowned at her phone.

"Oh, I dunno. I figured you'd drive back after dinner on Sunday."

Gabrielle nodded.

"Well, I'll leave you to it." Mrs. Johnson rose from the window seat. She stopped at the door and looked back. "I think it's time for a spring refresher. Redecorate in here a little. It can't stay my little girl's room forever."

"Yeah, sure." Gabrielle seemed unconcerned.

Mrs. Johnson watched her, a little sadly. "Maybe we can do lunch on Saturday. Pick out new décor and bedding together."

"Sounds good."

Mrs. Johnson sighed and left the room. Only later did she realize that Gabrielle never did talk to her about how she'd been spending her evenings.

"Something isn't right."

"Things couldn't be more right." Brandon watched Gabrielle from the bed, patting the space beside him. "Come back to bed."

Gabrielle frowned, pacing the hotel room. Where was her phone? If she could only find her phone, she could check her messages or her calendar. "There's someplace I'm supposed to be."

"Yeah, here. With me." Brandon rose from the bed and strode across the room to take Gabrielle in his arms. "It's so much easier if you don't fight it," he murmured into her ear as he nuzzled her neck. "Just let the dream take you."

six

SEAN LOOKED up in surprise when the doorbell rang on Sunday evening. Wearing only a pair of boxers, he reached for a rumpled shirt and left his room to see who was at the door. He raised an eyebrow as he looked through the peephole. Gabrielle stood on the porch, keys in hand, a duffle bag slung over her shoulder.

Sean opened the door. "Why didn't you just let yourself in?"

Gabrielle's eyes lit up at the sight of Sean before she glanced down at her keys. "I dunno, guess I wasn't thinking." Her lips curled up into a sly smile as she set down her bag to throw her arms around him.

Sean did not think anything of it when Gabrielle breathed in the scent of his freshly washed hair, but as the hug went on for moments longer than it should have, he became self-conscious of her warm body pressed against his own. Sean gently pushed her away. "Are you feeling okay, Bri?"

"I'm fine." She pouted, gazing at Sean from under her lowered lashes. "But you could help me feel better." She reached for the waistband of his boxers to pull him close.

"Woah." This time Sean pushed her away with more force.

"What's the matter?" Gabrielle tilted her head. "Oh, we're not...

you're not…" She paused, flustered. "I'm not your type," she finally finished, a look of understanding and disappointment flashing in her blue eyes. "Pity. I could always…"

Gabrielle went silent, biting her lip.

"Always what, Bri?"

Gabrielle shook her head, eyes darkening. "Never mind. I'm tired. Early call time in the morning."

Sean watched as she appeared to head into his room before shaking her head and entering the room beside it. He continued to watch as Gabrielle walked into her own room and closed the door, his brows knitting together in apprehension and growing dismay.

After a few minutes, Sean returned to his own room.

He locked the door.

A lot had surprised Sean in the last twelve hours, but not the note he found on the kitchen counter in the morning – except for the elegant swoop of the handwriting with which Gabrielle advised him that she planned to find somewhere else to stay. She didn't want him to worry—she just needed some time to herself.

Nice of her to leave a handwritten note instead of sending a text, Sean mused as he poured himself a bowl of cereal. He sat down to eat, checking his phone. No new messages from Gabrielle, but he did have a text from his ex, Monica. *Ugh*. But his annoyance faded when he saw that someone else had texted. A bartender he'd met the previous week. Sean grinned as he replied to Lance.

He paid no mind to the first headline in his social media feed about a self-help writer and influencer last seen in Syracuse and presumed missing.

Sean laid down on the couch after his shift at the coffee shop on campus. Though he'd booked work in the wardrobe department of the same film for which Gabrielle had left early that morning, his services were not needed until later this week. He wondered what he would say to her if they crossed paths.

Sean groaned when someone knocked on the door.

Gabrielle back for more of her things?

No.

When he looked out the peephole, he saw two official-looking men in dark glasses and suits: one who stood about six feet, with a blond buzz cut and broad muscles. The other was shorter, with dark hair and a mustache. Sean struggled to maintain a neutral expression as he opened the door with shaking fingers.

After confirming his identity, the men introduced themselves as "AgentBakerAgentMorris," or something of the sort. They flashed their badges as fast as they spoke, so fast Sean could only assume they worked for the FBI. "Can we come in?"

Sean ushered them into the apartment. He gestured to the chair and futon, but they remained standing. He ran a hand through his hair as he stood before them.

"Have you seen this woman?"

Agent Buzz Cut – Sean could not remember if he introduced himself as Baker or Morris - pulled out a photo of Gabrielle, demure in a baby blue tee shirt as she smiled at the camera.

Sean nodded. "That's Gabrielle Johnson. My roommate. Well, I mean she was my roommate." And his best friend, but it hurt too much to say so out loud. "She just got back from spring break last night, moved out early this morning." Agent Buzz Cut scrawled something on a notepad he produced from an inner pocket of his suit.

Sean waited for some sort of explanation, but Agent Mustache held a different photo in front of him. This photo showed an older blond woman – how old, Sean could not tell – smiling brightly in a designer suit. A professional headshot, he presumed. "What about this woman?"

"I've never seen her before in my life."

"Really? She's quite famous." Agent Buzz Cut looked doubtful.

"She's one of those...what do you call 'em?" He paused as he searched for the right word. "An influencer."

Agent Mustache rolled his eyes at his partner. "You didn't even know who she was until she went missing." He turned back to Sean. "You read a lot of self-help books, kid?"

Sean shrugged. "Not really, no."

Agent Mustache raised an eyebrow at his partner, vindicated.

Agent Buzz Cut ignored him. "She's been all over the evening news." He peered at Sean with steel blue eyes. "According to our records, Gabrielle Johnson is the last person to have seen her."

"I don't watch a lot of news, either." Sean shrugged again. "Sorry."

"Well, if you see Gabrielle again, have her give us a call." Agent Mustache pulled a card out of his pocket and handed it to Sean.

He was right.

FBI.

What had Gabrielle gotten herself into?

seven

SEAN REPORTED to the wardrobe department head on Wednesday. "You'll never believe who our first fitting is tonight." Hilary Taylor smirked at him as she adjusted her wire-rimmed glasses. "I mean, unless you've already heard, of course."

"C'mon, you know I don't get starstruck anymore."

"Oh, it's not a star." Hilary raised an eyebrow. "It's Gabrielle."

Sean's jaw dropped.

"So, you haven't heard. What's going on with you two? I heard a rumor that she moved out. And Chase said she was a mega-bitch at the production meeting on Monday, which does not sound like our Bri, but he says that about all the girls who won't date him. Next thing any of us knew, she scored a small part because someone had to drop the film. Guess they didn't want to bother with a casting call at the last minute."

"That *really* does not sound like Bri," Sean said, finally.

"Well, whatever happened between you two, keep it professional. She'll be here any minute." Hilary turned to steam some dresses on a rack. "You can start pulling dress shoes. Size six."

. . .

Hilary did not need to worry. Apart from a brief moment of surprise at seeing Sean in the wardrobe department, Gabrielle conducted herself with a cool politeness. If anything, someone might have described her as sweet, even demure—a far cry from the predatory seductress he'd encountered yesterday.

Still, seeing her try on an assortment of tops and dresses convinced Sean of one thing. This was not his Bri. And not just the way she filled out the clothes a little more than his roommate would have. While her shy smile evoked the real Gabrielle, the calculated cunning in her eyes gave her away as an imposter.

"See you around, Sean."

Gabrielle smiled, but the grin did not reach her eyes. She reached for a designer handbag Sean had not seen before today, sliding the chained strap over the shoulder of her form-fitting dress.

"Later, Bri."

"Wow," Hilary breathed after Gabrielle left. "You could feel the temperature drop five degrees when she saw you." She gave Sean a look of sympathy. "For what it's worth, you handled things well. I hope that whatever it was that happened between you two, you can work it out."

Sean nodded. He finished labeling hangers for Gabrielle's selected outfits, then prepared for the next fitting.

Sean only saw Gabrielle in passing over the next week and a half, but she was all anyone wanted to talk about in his presence.

"So how do you think she got the part, anyway? Think she slept with the director?" Jenna Mitchell, another wardrobe assistant, raised her well-defined eyebrows as her burgundy lips curved into a cruel smile during breakfast the following Friday.

"No way." Desiree Jackson, a production assistant with long black cornrows, shook her head. "I know she's been acting a little weird lately, but from what I heard, it was all on the up and up. She was in this production meeting with the casting department. It came up that a small part needed to be recast. When they decided to go with someone local, she asked Bryce if she could be considered for the role. He took a picture with his phone and filmed her delivering a few lines. The director loved her. More production hours for me, so I ain't mad about it."

"I heard she's been all over Mason Wright. Jack said he caught them making out in the hall between takes. I wonder if she knew who he was before filming started. I only just watched some clips of his soap online the other night. Crazy stuff. Maybe he's the reason for her sudden interest in performing." Jenna turned to Sean. "She's your roommate. So, tell us - does she have posters of Mason Wright plastered all over her room? Is she writing their names together on all of her notebooks?"

"She moved out last week, remember?" Sean took another bite of his breakfast sandwich and checked his phone.

"Oh, right." Jenna feigned a contrite expression as she met Desiree's annoyed glare across the table. "Well, I should get back to the trailer. Later."

"I swear, that girl missed her calling as a gossip columnist or TMZ reporter or something." Desiree offered Sean an encouraging smile. "For what it's worth, I don't think Bri's been as bad as all that. I know you two are having problems, but she's still your friend. Jenna should respect that."

Sean shrugged. "She's curious. I get it. I don't think any of us really knows what's going on."

And only I seem to know it isn't her.

That night, Sean received a phone call from an unknown number with a Syracuse area code. Gabrielle? *His* Gabrielle?

"Hello?"

"This is Mrs. Johnson. Gabrielle's mother. Is this Sean?"

"Yes, it's me..."

"Is Gabrielle there with you now? I've been trying to reach her, but she won't answer her phone, and these people came, and they asked us all these questions, and I'm really worried about her."

"Gabrielle moved out last week. I've only seen her at work, but we really haven't talked. Who came by to see you? When?"

"Earlier this week. I think they were with the FBI?" The way she said it signaled to Sean that Mr. Johnson was beside her. "They kept asking about that missing writer. Simone Weaver? Said Gabrielle was the last person to see her."

"Yeah, someone came to see me, too. After Gabrielle had already gone." Sean did not mention they'd questioned him over a week ago. He did not know what it meant that they came to him first.

"Oh, Sean, if you see her again, please tell her to call me."

"Of course."

Sean looked at his phone. Then he rose from the couch, shoving the phone into his back pocket. He pulled a windbreaker off the coat hook and slipped it on as he left the apartment.

"Hey, you."

Sean could not hear Lance over the music, but he had no problems reading his lips. He had spent a lot of time studying those lips the last week or so. Sean forced himself to meet Lance's curious gaze as he pulled out an empty seat at the bar.

"You okay?"

Sean did not need to read Lance's lips this time. Lance leaned over to set down a napkin in front of Sean. The bartender's brows furrowed as his hazel eyes searched Sean's face. He had pale blond hair and warm brown skin, and he was the most beautiful man Sean had ever seen – and Sean had once dressed an actor whom a magazine crowned "Sexiest Man Alive."

"Yeah, the whole Bri thing just has me down. Her mom called me tonight." Sean watched as Lance mixed bourbon, lemon juice, and sugar in a steel jigger. "I guess the Feds came by tonight to talk to her about Simone Weaver."

"That author who went missing?" Lance poured the drink into a glass he set on the napkin, garnishing it with a maraschino cherry and orange peel. "Did Gabrielle say anything about it?"

"Not to me." Sean's frown deepened. "I don't even know if she's talked to the FBI, but they must've questioned her by now." He picked up the glass to take a drink.

"Seems likely. Are things still strained between the two of you?"

Sean shrugged. "She's like a stranger to me now."

"Anything I can do to help?"

"Yeah, if you could find the real Bri Johnson and bring her home, that would be great." Sean reached for his drink to take another sip, but Lance grabbed his free hand and gave it a squeeze. Sean gazed up at him, his troubles forgotten for the moment.

eight

GABRIELLE'S WRIST TICKLED. She tried to brush off whatever she felt nuzzling against her flesh, eyes still closed.

"Brandon, stop it." Gabrielle giggled as he worked his way up her arm to her neck with feather-light kisses. "I'm not in the mood." She gave him a half-hearted shove.

He grasped both wrists and held them above her head as he burrowed his face deeper into her neck. "You're always in the mood."

"Get off of her, you miserable beasts!"

Gabrielle heard a smooth yet commanding voice but did not recognize the language. She struggled to open her eyes. The air suddenly felt cool against her neck and arms. She sensed wetness and shivered. Something – no, several somethings - skittered away from her body, hissing and mewling in anger and disappointment.

"Go on. Go! Before I kill the damn lot of you!"

. . .

"I mean it, Brandon. This isn't right."

Gabrielle struggled against him, but when he raised his head, she found herself staring not at Brandon, but Chase, his lips curled into a cruel grimace as he snarled at her in some foreign tongue and lifted her from the bed.

Gabrielle felt herself being carried over rough terrain by strong, muscular arms. Her back ached, and liquid trickled down from her neck and the insides of her arms and wrists, warm at first but cooling quickly in the evening chill. She opened her eyes, staring up into a night sky filled with unfamiliar constellations and waves of green and magenta light, but only for a moment before her heavy eyelids drooped again.

"Just hang in there. Almost home."

That same unfamiliar voice and language. Gabrielle opened her eyes and looked toward a large dark tree with gnarled branches and an eerie phosphorescent glow. Then she turned her head to look up at her rescue.

What she saw made her scream.

Then, merciful darkness.

nine

"WHAT IN THE HELL?"

"How d'you suppose she ended up here?"

"I dunno, maybe she was hiking?"

"Dressed like that? And what the hell happened to her neck'n arms?"

"Mosquitos?"

"That's a helluva lotta blood for mosquito bites."

"Really *big* mosquitos?"

"We should call the police. Check her for a pulse."

"Nnn..."

"Did she just talk. What's she sayin'?"

"N-No...police."

Gabrielle's eyes fluttered open. She squinted up at two middle-aged men in hunting gear, one tall and thin, the other short with a bit of a beer belly. The sun hung low in the sky to the east, which meant it must be early morning. The memory of an alien nightscape came to Gabrielle, but she pushed the image out of her mind to focus on the present circumstances.

"Miss, you're awfully hurt. At the very least, you need to be checked out by the paramedics or something." The taller of the two men lifted his hat to scratch at his hair. Deep lines creased his fore-head. He exchanged a look of doubt and distrust with his companion.

Gabrielle forced herself to sit up, feeling lightheaded as she leaned over her knees. She held back a gasp of pain as sensation slowly returned to her limbs. "It's not as bad as it looks, I swear," she told them in a hoarse voice even though she had no idea how it looked or how bad it was. Gabrielle looked down at her arms and saw her once-white shirt stained with blood, some fresh. She closed her eyes for a moment to steady herself.

"You weren't doing drugs or something, were you?"

Gabrielle opened her eyes and glared. "Do I look like..." she started to ask, then stopped herself. "No, I...I just got lost somehow," she continued, softening her tone. "I don't know what happened to my arms, but I don't do drugs."

"I still don't like this." The tall man fiddled with his phone.

"Can I call a friend?" Gabrielle tried to give him what she hoped was her most plaintive but lucid look.

"Just let her call her friend, Joe. I told Jules I'd be back in time for brunch with her mother."

Joe glared at the shorter man before handing Gabrielle his phone. She murmured her thanks, then stared down at the screen, trying to remember Sean's number as something other than "Sean" Joe's frown lines deepened as he watched. After another uncomfortable moment, the number came to her, and Gabrielle began to dial. The phone rang several times. She was about to give up when a husky voice answered.

"Hello?"

"Sean? It's Bri."

"Bri? Where are you?"

"I'm..." Gabrielle paused. She looked at the hunters with a rueful expression. "Where are we?"

"About thirty minutes out of Rochester," the shorter man answered.

Gabrielle blinked in surprise. "About thirty minutes out of Rochester," she repeated into the phone. No way would Sean be willing to pick her up and drive her all the way back to her parents in Syracuse, but she could not imagine calling her parents instead.

"Is there somewhere we can meet?"

Relieved, Gabrielle looked at the hunters again. "Would you be willing to drop me off someplace my friend can get me?"

"There's a diner we like to go to just as you get back into town," Joe said. He gave Gabrielle the address. She repeated it to Sean.

"I'll get there as soon as I can."

Gabrielle frowned as she returned the phone to Joe. Sean sounded terse, anxious even. She wondered how long she'd been missing, but she didn't want to ask, at the risk of Joe deciding to call the police after all. At least there hadn't been a missing person report yet, or if there was, they had not seen it before finding her.

Gabrielle remembered the shorter man saying something about brunch. She had gone missing on a Sunday.

Had it really been a whole week since her meeting with Simone?

"Not sure about bringing you back to civilization all bloodied up like that, but I might have something you can wear back in the truck." Joe leaned down to pick up the carcass of a wild turkey Gabrielle had not noticed until now. "At least we caught one," he told the other man as they gathered the rest of their things.

Joe pulled a bottle of water from his pack, offering it to Gabrielle. Gabrielle forced herself to drink slowly. The cold liquid hurt her raw throat, and she knew she could become ill if she guzzled. She followed the hunters through the woods, shivering as she hugged herself tightly. Only now did she realize how tired she was, and how hungry. Her stomach rumbled.

The shorter man pulled a granola bar out of his back pocket. "That should tide you over until we get to Paula's Place."

Gabrielle accepted the granola bar with her free hand. She tucked the water bottle under her arm to open it, pleased with her coordination. Her limbs no longer prickled from waking, but her back still ached and the wounds under her shirt felt tender to the touch.

Itchy, too.

The granola bar was warm and squishy with melted bits of chocolate from being in the man's pocket, but Gabrielle felt too ravenous to mind. She ate as they walked, grateful to feel solid ground beneath her feet and the warmth of the rising sun on her face. Birds called to each other overhead, and squirrels and chipmunks chittered as they ran away through the underbrush.

Gabrielle sat in a booth at the small diner, wearing an oversized flannel shirt over her bloodied blouse. Joe insisted she keep it. He also insisted on buying Gabrielle breakfast before he left with his friend. For her part, the server did not ask too many questions as she served a plate full of eggs, toast, and hash browns.

Gabrielle ate in silence, watching the front door of the diner. She was on her second cup of coffee when Sean walked in. "That's my ride," she told the server. "Thank Joe again for me the next time he comes in."

Outside, she told Sean, "You must've hauled ass to get here. It didn't feel like it took us all that long to walk out of the woods to Joe's truck." She squeaked in pain and surprise when Sean pulled her into a tight hug.

"I'm sorry." Sean loosened his grip. Now he held Gabrielle at arm's length while he peered into her eyes. "Are you hurt? What happened to you?"

"Let's get in the car. I'll tell you what I can on the way to my parents'. I can't believe you're willing to do this for me."

"Your parents? Why? They don't even know..." Sean's voice trailed off as they walked to his car, a gold Malibu that was starting to rust, another casualty of winter weather and the salt used to melt ice and snow. He opened the passenger door for Gabrielle before getting in on the driver's side.

"Know what? That I'm here even though my car is still there? Ugh. They're going to have so many questions. I don't know what to tell them. I don't even know how long I've been missing. It's only been a week, right?"

Sean turned to gaze at her, his expression troubled. "Your car isn't there, Bri. You drove it back when spring break ended. Two weeks ago."

Gabrielle sat in stunned silence as he started to drive. Sean did not speak again until he turned onto the highway.

"What is the last thing you remember?"

"I had a meeting with this woman. Simone Weaver?"

Sean stiffened.

"You've heard of her? She writes self-help books. My mom made me set up the appointment."

"Simone Weaver has been missing for about as long as you were...wherever you've been. I saw it on the news. And someone came by the apartment wanting to speak to you – a couple of federal agents, actually - but I hadn't seen you since you moved out that morning, until you showed up at work the next week."

"I – I mean, she - moved out?"

"After you came home from your parents and you – she - tried to grope me. That's when I knew it couldn't be you. Bri, what happened when you met with Simone Weaver?"

Gabrielle's blood ran cold.

"You wouldn't believe me if I told you."

"Try me. I'm feeling weirdly open-minded at the moment."

Gabrielle took a deep breath. "She wanted to meet me at her hotel room. It was stupid, I know. She gave me this strange tea and started asking me questions. Then I started to feel weird. I saw... things. I guess she must have drugged me or something."

"What did you see?"

"Me. She turned into me. "

ten

BY THE TIME they arrived at the apartment, Gabrielle and Sean had come to a couple conclusions: Simone Weaver had assumed her identity and appearance, and now Gabrielle needed to lay low until they figured out the "how" and the "why." She dozed most of the drive home.

Sean insisted Gabrielle take a shower and relax before they delved any deeper into the mystery. She did not remove Joe's flannel shirt until she shut the bathroom door. Then she peeled off her own shirt, which clung to the dried blood that encrusted her arms. Only the dusty jeans would be salvageable after she washed them.

Gabrielle stared at her reflection in the mirror. She noted how pale her skin appeared, even for a fair redhead, and the deep shadows beneath her haunted blue eyes. No wonder Joe had been so reluctant to abandon his idea of calling the police.

Gabrielle crumpled up the shirt and pushed it into the garbage.

Another memory came back to her as she leaned forward to observe the wounds on her neck and arms. It wasn't a vision so much as the sensation of pressure against her skin and a brief sting fading into a dull ache until it had gone. Then, she'd felt nothing but cold air and wet blood.

Gabrielle shuddered. "What *were* those things?"

Her reflection did not answer. Instead, her eyes widened. She swooned under the full weight of the recognition that things, living things, had been feeding on her, like leeches or...

Vampires?

Really big mosquitoes.

Gabrielle turned the shower on high and let the hot water pour over her, even as her mother's voice cautioned her against washing her hair with hot water. Frizz was the least of her concerns.

Gabrielle washed the blood from her arms and neck. She did not see any streaks of red traveling from her wounds to her heart, but that only ruled out blood poisoning. Otherwise, she had no way of knowing what sort of toxins and diseases she'd been exposed to, or even what to do about it if she had.

Gabrielle giggled as she considered walking into an urgent care and saying, *"Hey, doc, I got bit by some sort of evil little vampire things in another world, and I wanted you to find out if they gave me any alien diseases."* They'd lock her away for sure.

After she stepped out of the shower and wrapped her body with a fluffy blue bath sheet, Gabrielle covered her wounds with antibiotic cream. She winced as she counted over a dozen pairs of puncture marks. Gabrielle decided to keep that part of the story to herself as she slipped into a plush baby blue bathrobe.

While his own experiences may have left Sean with no choice but to accept the reality of her apparent doppelgänger, accepting the existence of another world of small vampiric creatures seemed like too much for Gabrielle to ask of him.

Gabrielle ran a comb through her hair to detangle it, then went into her bedroom. She opened her cherry red dresser. Nothing appeared to be missing. Gabrielle pulled out underwear, a black tank top, and a pair of soft black, blue, and green plaid pajama pants. She dressed, then looked at her wounded arms. Gabrielle pulled an oversized heather gray hoodie off a hanger in her closet and put it on.

At least Simone Weaver, or whatever her real name was, had left most of Gabrielle's belongings, including a bag full of the clothes her mother had purchased that fateful Saturday before her disappearance. *She must not be a fan of business casual*, Gabrielle decided. She fell back into a pile of fuzzy blue, pink, and purple throw pillows on her still-made bed. Even her laptop appeared untouched on her small wooden desk across the room.

On a whim, Gabrielle jumped off the bed to do a search for people who could steal someone else's appearance. The closest thing she could find was the metaphysical definition of a doppelgänger from a German story: a paranormal entity like a spirit or a wraith that looked identical to a living person. The imposter must have felt real enough to Sean when she grabbed him, but it was as good a descriptor as any.

Gabrielle considered checking her email, but the mere thought exhausted her, so she decided to rejoin her roommate in the living room instead. She sat in a tan armchair with plush oversized cushions across from Sean, who sat on the futon. He looked up from his phone to regard Gabrielle with a tender look of concern. She noticed his own eyes were shadowed but nowhere near as severely as hers were.

"She has your car, your phone, and your wallet. That makes things tricky. I can pay your share of the rent this month, so don't worry about that. I ordered takeout, by the way. Should be here any minute." Sean gave Gabrielle another look of concern as she sat on the couch. "Wings from Nickel City Grill. Mild instead of medium. An order of fries, too. I hope that's okay?"

"That sounds great." Gabrielle tried to force a smile, but she remembered something else. "Oh, no. Production was going to start as soon as I came home from break."

"Yeah, about that…"

"Is she working? She blew it off, didn't she? Do you even know?"

"Oh, she's working on the movie."

"Why do you say it like that?" Gabrielle narrowed her eyes as she regarded her roommate. "Sean…?"

"An actress got sick and had to bow out at the last minute. She wormed her way into getting the part. So, I guess she's not working *on* so much as *in* the movie." Sean gave a rueful grin.

"Figures. She seemed pretty hyper about acting when I told her I worked in the film industry. I guess the self-help industry wasn't satiating her desire for attention."

"Well, she still wants to be an influencer, too, if your social media is any indication. Oh yeah, you have a lot more followers now. Like, *a lot* a lot. Total rebranding."

"Oh, no." Gabrielle buried her face in her hands.

"It's not as bad as all that. Just a few selfies, girl-next-door-type stuff, and one black and white that was maybe a little sultry, but not, like, overtly sexual. Oh, and she vaguebooked once. No idea about private messages, but I get the impression she's pretty fixated on the film, so you have that going for you...sort of, in a way, I guess. Your advisor's been trying to reach you, though. And your mom."

Gabrielle jumped when his phone rang. "Who's that?"

"*Not* your mom." Sean's lips curved into a half-smile. "Lance's one of those old-fashioned weirdos who'd rather call than text." The affection in his voice indicated he did not mind. "Lance, hi. Hey, can I call you back? Bri...she...she's home. We're talking through some stuff. Talk to you in a bit." His smile widened.

"Lance?" Gabrielle raised an eyebrow, grinning.

"Yeah, I met him over break. He bartends at The Loft. It's this new upscale lounge downtown. You'd like it. Dark. Soft music. Lots of places to sit and talk. Artsy types like to get together there to discuss projects and things over drinks. I think I spent over an hour talking to Lance at the bar after closing the first night."

"Any pictures?"

Sean pulled one up on his phone and handed it to Gabrielle.

"Wow..."

"Right?"

Gabrielle stared down at a lean, muscular man in a black V-neck shirt leaning forward with his hands on the counter of a bar. He had close cropped tufts of white-blond hair, hazel eyes, high cheekbones, and the most flawless brown skin she had ever seen.

Gabrielle shivered.

"Are you okay?"

"Yeah, I'm fine. I just...I'm glad one of us enjoyed spring break."

"Oh, Bri. I'm sorry. We'll figure this out."

Someone knocked on the door.

Sean rose to answer. "That must be our food." He patted Gabrielle on the knee as he walked by. "The important thing is that you're home. And safe."

After Gabrielle ate, she went back to her room and turned on her laptop to check her email. Much like her bedroom, the account she used for school appeared largely untouched. She had a few unread emails from classmates and teachers, and several from her advisor. The most recent warned her of being dropped from her classes.

Gabrielle wanted to reply to the email, but she worried her doppelgänger might see it. She would just have to sort everything out in person tomorrow. At least she seemed unlikely to encounter her doppelgänger on campus, but that was little consolation if it came at the expense of her grades or worse, her enrollment.

And then there was the FBI to worry about. She remembered what Sean said about federal agents. They couldn't possibly think she had something to do with Simone Weaver's disappearance, could they?

They'd even contacted her parents.

Her parents.

Gabrielle cringed when she thought of speaking to her mother, but she knew she could not avoid her parents forever. She shut down her laptop and walked back into the living room to borrow Sean's phone.

"I don't know what's gotten into you lately, between your behavior over break, staying out all night doing who knows what, to ignoring our calls since you've been back in Buffalo. Your father and I have been so worried about you. And now the FBI is asking questions. I told them you obviously didn't have anything to do with that flaky Simone Weaver disappearing, but people are starting to talk. And now I hear you're starring in some movie?"

Gabrielle leaned back against a pile of pillows on her bed, her eyes closed as she waited for a chance to speak.

"Honestly, Bri."

"Bri?"

"Bri, are you still there?"

Gabrielle opened her eyes.

"Sorry, Mom. I've just been really busy, you know, with the movie and school and everything. It's just a small role, though. Barely worth mentioning. Thought it might be a good learning experience, you know, to get a sense of how it feels on the other side of the camera?"

Her mother did not say anything, for a refreshing change, so Gabrielle continued. "I don't know what to tell you about the FBI. Probably just covering all their bases, or whatever. And you're right that obviously, I had nothing to do with Simone Weaver's disappearance."

You're the one who made me meet with that thing.

Gabrielle bit her lip on that particular sentiment. Instead, she said, "You don't need to worry about me, I promise."

"I don't know, Bri." Mrs. Johnson went quiet for a few more moments. "I think we need to have another serious discussion about your plans this summer," she finally said.

"I'm sorry I've been a little weird the last few weeks, but me..." Gabrielle tried to say.

"It has been a lot more than just the last few weeks, Bri," her mother interrupted, "but don't even get me started on the whole Brandon thing."

Gabrielle sat up straight. "*What* whole Brandon thing?" she asked slowly. Her brow furrowed.

"Oh, don't play coy with me," Mrs. Johnson said. "He's been trying to get a hold of you, too. I know something happened between you even if you don't want to talk to me about it. I just hope you had the presence of mind to be careful."

Gabrielle shuddered. A hazy memory of Brandon in Simone's hotel room came back to her, but that could not be right. She had not seen him since that dinner. Had her doppelgänger done something?

Was it *her memory* in Gabrielle's dreams?

"Bri? Bri!"

Gabrielle rubbed at her face, then ran her hand through her hair. "Sorry, tired. Been a busy weekend, and I have a lot of things I need to do before school tomorrow."

"Fine." Then, in a softer tone: "Your father and I love you very much, Bri. I just want you to know that."

"I know. Love you, too."

"Stay safe."

"Always."

eleven

"SEAN, have I ever talked to you about this guy I went to high school with, Brandon Williams?" Gabrielle spread cream cheese on a bagel and took a bite.

Sean thought, stirring cream and sugar into a cup of coffee. "I don't think so, but you've never talked a lot about high school."

"He's this jock. Usually, he just ignored me. We, uhm...we didn't exactly hang with the same crowds." In truth, Gabrielle did not run with any crowd in high school, but she had little interest in reliving her teen angst. "When we did interact, it...wasn't great. He was kind of a bully, to be honest, but I had to go to dinner with him and his awful family when I was home for spring break. My mom asked him to take me on a campus tour. She wants me to come home senior year."

"What?" Sean looked up from his coffee. "Why?"

Gabrielle rolled her eyes. "Don't even get me started. Anyway, I think maybe my doppelgänger took him up on that tour, and something happened between them."

"The kind of something that would interest our friends from the FBI?" Sean took a sip of his coffee.

"*Different* kind of something." Gabrielle grimaced.

"Oh." Sean took another sip, then coughed. "Oh!"

"Yeah." Gabrielle set her bagel down next to her laptop on the kitchen counter. She opened her school email and gasped. "Speak of the proverbial devil," she said, turning to Sean.

"Which one?"

"Brandon." Gabrielle pointed to a message in her inbox. "Read it for me. I can't look. How did he even find my email?"

"Easy enough to find in the student directory."

Sean clicked on the email. He started to read.

"Oh. Oh, wow."

"What?"

Sean tried to close the lid, but Gabrielle pulled the laptop from him. She began to read, her eyes widening as her mouth dropped. "'The things you did to me'...what things?" She covered her face with her hands. "Oh, God, Sean, I think he's seen me...I mean *her* naked."

Sean's forehead wrinkled. "How would she know...I mean – how, like, *anatomically accurate* do you think she is?"

Gabrielle stared at him, horrified. "You know what. Never mind. She can have my life. I don't want it anymore."

Sean squeezed her shoulder. "Whatever happened between them, it doesn't matter. She's not *you*. Look on the bright side, at least she didn't take over your actual body."

"Small comfort," Gabrielle said.

"I'm going to delete the email and block him from contacting you ever again." Sean turned around to manage her account settings. "Just a hunch, but I bet he's had plenty of experience with ghosting on the other end of things. Think of all the scorned lovers you're avenging." Sean gave her a reassuring grin as he closed the laptop. "Finish your bagel and get ready."

"She doesn't have any nude scenes, does she?" Gabrielle asked.

Sean laughed. "It's not that kind of movie."

. . .

Talking to her advisor before class was a piece of cake compared to listening to her mother last night. For all her curt emails, Constance Moore was more worried than angry, all nervous energy and fleeting smiles mixed with the occasional grimace.

The woman pushed frizzy brown hair out of her face as she looked at her computer. "You've always been such a strong student, this semester should be salvageable as long as you don't miss any more classes, but it's really up to your teachers how to proceed." Constance removed her reading glasses and set them on her desk, turning her chair to face Gabrielle.

"Professor Landon is pretty relaxed, and I don't know if Professor Hill even takes attendance during her lectures and screenings. But you missed a couple of the smaller discussion group sessions, and I can't imagine D'Andre is happy about your extended absence, either. You know how grad students can be. When's your next meeting with Professor Smith? For your independent study?"

"Not for another couple of weeks. I'm supposed to have a rough draft of my research paper ready for her." Gabrielle chose not to mention she'd barely written more than a couple pages of her essay, *Strong Female Protagonist: Evolving Representations of Women in Modern Media*, before spring break.

"Good, good." Constance put her glasses back on and glanced at the clock. "Looks like you have about ten minutes before class. You don't want to be late."

Gabrielle took that as her cue to leave, shouldering her backpack as she walked out of the guidance office. She shivered as a gust of cold wind penetrated her heavy sweatshirt. Gray clouds churned in the sky overhead as she hurried across campus.

* * *

"Well, well, well. Look what the cat dragged in." Andrew Blake, one of the teaching assistants for Professor Hill's cinematic history class, gazed at Gabrielle over his wire-framed glasses. He reclined in a leather chair at the back of the class with his hands behind his head and his feet propped up on a desk.

"Who even says that anymore?" Sean's ex-girlfriend, Monica Hill, gave Andrew a look of disdain, twisting her long blond hair into a messy bun that somehow appeared both artful and fabulous. She did not even glance at Gabrielle, who had no choice but to sit down beside her in the last available seat.

"Me, just now. Obviously." Andrew put his feet down and rolled his chair closer to the desks arranged in a circle around the room. "Anybody want to fill Bri in on what she missed while she was busy living it up with her new Hollywood friends?"

"Yeah," said another student with a smirk. "You told us everything we needed to know for the final and made us promise not to tell Bri if she bothered coming back to school."

Gabrielle rolled her eyes at Darren Lopez, who ran a hand through his spiky black hair and laughed. She pulled out her notebook and a pencil as the class continued with its familiar banter and discussion of last week's screening.

One thing Gabrielle had to say for Andrew, the amiable teacher's assistant was one of the less self-important grad students she dealt with at school, and he always covered whatever material they needed to know for tests in their weekly discussion groups. She doubted she was the only no-show at last Friday's screening for that very reason.

D'Andre Jones was every bit the self-important grad student Andrew was not, but he was also talented and professional, unlike a certain assistant director Gabrielle knew. So she approached him with a certain grudging respect before her production class that afternoon.

"You know, class isn't over just because we're done filming our shorts," he said, barely glancing up from his laptop. "We still need to plan and schedule our screening, and this year I want to keep the social media component. Stream it live, all that good stuff. Nice work on 'The Game' by the way. I've seen an early cut, and it's looking pretty good. You should direct more often."

Gabrielle felt her cheeks heat from the unexpected compliment.

D'Andre closed his laptop and leaned back in his chair. He looked at her, considering. "Unless you decide you like it better in front of the camera, that is."

Gabrielle's blush deepened. "No way. You know that isn't me."

"Neither is missing two weeks of school, but here we are." A smile tugged at the corner of D'Andre's lips.

"Yeah, it's kind of a weird time in my life." Gabrielle offered a rueful grin. "I'm working on it."

"Well, get it together."

As other students arrived and they discussed food and venues for the screening of their short films, Gabrielle relished the return to normalcy. For the moment she allowed herself to forget the Gabrielle-sized problem that loomed before her. At least she did not have to worry about running into her doppelgänger here. The real test would be when she visited the movie set tomorrow.

twelve

"I REALLY DON'T THINK this is a good idea." Sean opened the passenger side door of his car, a used grey Malibu.

Gabrielle sat down. "I just want to get a sense of how things are going for myself."

Sean looked doubtful as he closed the door.

"Besides," she continued as he got in on the driver's side, "you said she had a later call time today. I'm not ready to alert her to my return. We don't even know who...I mean, *what* she is yet."

"Still sounds like a recipe for disaster, especially if anyone says anything to tip her off. Plus, Chase is back in town because they needed to hire another second AD for *A New Man*."

Gabrielle winced at the mention of his name, but he was the least of her concerns. "Are you sure you'll be done before the store closes? I want to get this phone problem sorted out, even if I can't access any of my social media yet."

"Yeah. I already talked to the store about setting up one of those friends and family plans, too. It might even save us both some money." Sean paused, pensive. "I mean, apart from whatever money she's been blowing through in your bank account."

"That's the weird thing." Gabrielle turned to look at him. "I checked online, and it's all still there. I mean, obviously she must have plenty of money squirreled away from her life as Simone Weaver. I guess siphoning from my account hasn't been worth the bother. Not yet, anyway. At least I found that emergency credit card in my dresser, so I have that until I can replace my debit card...and figure out what to do about her in case she's watching the account." Gabrielle groaned, closing her eyes as she massaged her temples. "God, what a mess."

"You know what?" Sean turned to look at her, his eyes widening. "I bet Simone Weaver wasn't even her first identity. For all we know, she's been around a *long* time."

"Wow." Gabrielle leaned her head against the headrest. "FBI. Doppelgängers. I can't believe this is my life now. Do you think they've talked to her? Those agents, I mean. They must have."

"Dunno. For your sake, let's just hope they never show up at work." Sean pulled into the parking lot of a building being used for the film shoot. "I'll meet you at the computer lab around five."

Gabrielle climbed out of the car, resolute.

Desiree looked up from the desk. Her jaw dropped at the sight of Gabrielle. She cupped a hand over the receiver of her headset, then hissed, "Bri - you were supposed to be through hair and makeup over an hour ago. You'd better haul ass before we both catch it from Chase. He is *not* in a good mood today."

"He's never in a good mood." The words slipped out before Gabrielle even had time to think.

Desiree laughed, then shooed Gabrielle away as she talked into her headset. "Hey, Cam? Bri's here."

Gabrielle left the room but stood just beyond the door, where she wouldn't be seen as she listened in.

"You're kidding?" Desiree glanced up, confirming that Gabrielle was out of earshot before she added, "Well, she needs one hell of a touch-up before she goes on set. She's lookin' rough."

Oh, no.

Sean must have gotten the doppelgänger's call time wrong. Now that she confirmed his story, Gabrielle considered leaving before anyone suspected anything was up, especially the doppelgänger. She'd started to head for the exit when someone grabbed her waist from behind and brushed aside her hair to kiss her neck.

"And just where do you think you're going?" The unfamiliar voice had a distinct foreign accent Gabrielle could not place. Australian, maybe? The speaker turned her around to kiss her full on the lips. His own lips were soft. Still in shock, she leaned into the kiss for a moment before pushing him away.

"What's wrong?" Taken aback, the bemused actor narrowed his eyes. "I thought you liked surprises, or is that only—".

He went silent, his warm brown eyes widening. Gabrielle noted his chiseled features and neatly styled light brown hair. An actor. Not an extra. Obviously not local. Definitely leading man material. And right now, his smooth persona was dropping as he took a step back. "I'm so sorry. I thought – you look just like her."

"That's not Gabrielle. I mean, she's not me. I'm Gabrielle. She —"- Gabrielle faltered. "We're twins. We, uhm, we didn't grow up together, but now she's back, and she's pretending to be me. It's... really complicated."

The actor nodded slowly, unconvinced. "And I thought the story-lines on my soap were convoluted."

Gabrielle saw activity behind him. It was her, the doppelgänger, wearing the kind of slinky dress that telegraphed *villainess*. A makeup artist with a side-swept splash of electric blue hair ushered her into a room at the end of the hall. "I don't know what Desiree was on about. You look gorgeous," Gabrielle heard them say.

The actor turned to look, but Gabrielle grabbed his arm before he saw the doppelgänger. "You can't tell her I was here. Promise you won't say anything?"

He held up his hands, bewildered, as he tried to process this new information. Gabrielle gave him one last pleading look before she rushed out of the building. She walked quickly to the nearest bus stop.

Gabrielle was about to enter the computer lab when someone called her name. She turned to see Sean's ex-girlfriend striding toward her. Monica's blond hair fell in loose curls over her shoulders, one of which was fashionably exposed by the pale rose sweater that accentuated her generous curves.

"So, I guess it's really over now, huh." Monica's high cheekbones flushed with anger. "What, did it stop being fun with me out of the picture? Or did you decide you no longer needed him once you found someone better to throw yourself at?"

Gabrielle stared at her, not understanding. A couple students stopped to watch with interest as Monica continued her tirade. She glared at them until they continued moving.

"Drop the innocent doe-eyed routine," Monica said, as though she had been practicing this speech for a while. "I always knew you two would be more than friends when Sean let you move in last year. He always denied it, but then we broke up, and you left, and it was so obvious I was right all along."

"Is that why...but I thought...wait, you thought he and I...?" Gabrielle shook her head as she tried to wrap her brain around the accusation. "Monica, he and I have only ever been friends. Wait a minute," she continued, her eyes narrowing, "didn't you che...?"

Monica narrowed her hazel eyes. "He already had one foot out the door. It didn't seem to matter much what I did." Even her sigh appeared rehearsed as she looked away.

Sometimes Gabrielle wondered what Sean had seen in Monica, apart from the beautiful hair and perfect figure, but he always assured her that she was different when she let her guard down. Sweet and funny, even a little goofy. Gabrielle found it hard to imagine her being sweet, let alone goofy, but she saw a hint of real vulnerability when Monica continued to speak.

70

"Anyway, it sounds like he's moving on to somebody else now." She frowned with genuine regret and disappointment.

Gabrielle nodded. "Lance. He told me. We're still friends, Monica. I've just been going through some things on my own that I'm trying to sort out..."

"You and me both." Monica turned abruptly and walked away.

Gabrielle watched her go. She always wondered why Monica never showed any interest in acting. She was a talented makeup artist, but the camera loved her, and she definitely did not lack for dramatic flair. That Monica ever considered Gabrielle a threat, well... she had to laugh.

Gabrielle had fallen into an easy friendship with Sean from the first time they sat next to each other in a screening for her introduction to film class. He was a year ahead of her in college, and he took her under his wing as she struggled to navigate her first year away from home. Any sexual tension was purely imagined on Monica's part. Sean was smart and funny and one of the most beautiful people she knew, but for whatever reason he did not trigger butterflies in her stomach like...

Mason

...anyone she'd dated in college - though, to be honest, most of them did not give her butterflies, or anything else, either.

And Gabrielle knew Sean felt nothing more than brotherly affection for her. Of course, if she had a real older brother, she mused, he'd probably be as bossy as her mother or as indifferent as her father. She was offended that Monica tried to cheapen her treasured bond with Sean. Sometimes he felt more like family than her actual family.

"Hey, are you going in...?"

A student stood with the door to the lab open, looking at Gabrielle from under his baseball cap as though he felt worried that she might bite.

"What? Oh, sorry. Just lost in my thoughts. Thanks." Gabrielle felt herself blushing as she walked past him into the lab. She forced herself to focus on her research paper as she sat in front of a computer and logged into her account.

"Wow, you made it all the way to the third page. Good job!"

A hand clapped Gabrielle on the back. She jumped, then turned to glare at Sean. "Like I can focus on a research paper at a time like this." She saved her file and logged out of her account. "You won't believe what happened today."

"Shh," someone hissed from another row of computers.

Gabrielle rolled her eyes at Sean. Then she made a beeline for the door of the computer lab.

Sean followed. "Let me guess," he said once they stepped outside of the lab. "A certain handsome Kiwi with beautiful green eyes tried to make out with the wrong Bri? I'd believe it."

"Kiwi? New Zealand? Is *that* where he's from?" Gabrielle stopped walking to stare at Sean. "Wait, how did you...?"

"Know?" Sean's wolfish grin widened. "*He* told me. After he asked me if I knew where to find you. Girl, you're lucky I'm the only one he talked to about this. Assuming he listens to me and doesn't talk to anyone else." He headed to the parking garage.

"You didn't tell me she was seeing anyone." Gabrielle glared at him as they walked.

Sean shrugged. "I've heard talk, but I didn't know anything solid. Until now, anyway."

Gabrielle looked away from Sean as they neared the garage, her annoyance fading. "You know the weird thing?"

"Weirder than...?" Sean held his arms out wide in a general indication of everything.

Gabrielle ignored his gesture, still staring into space. "My own parents couldn't tell the difference, but he could. Like, almost immediately."

"So did I."

Gabrielle's pensive gaze returned to Sean. "You're my best friend. He only just met me."

A slow grin spread across Sean's face. "You're starstruck."

Gabrielle rolled her eyes. "You know I don't care about that stuff."

"Okay, fine. But you're definitely into him." Sean led Gabrielle to a set of stairs leading up to the second floor of the parking garbage. He turned back to Gabrielle when they reached the top. "So, tell me." his eyes sparkled. "What was the kiss like? I mean, really?"

"Like a kiss meant for someone else." Gabrielle felt her cheeks grow warm at the memory of his lips pressed against hers.

"Aw, look on the bright side." Sean stopped beside his car, opening the passenger door for Gabrielle. "The next time he kisses her, I bet he's going to be thinking of you instead of kissing you and thinking about her."

Gabrielle's blush deepened as she sat down. "There might not even be a next time if he doesn't keep quiet about me. Ugh, this is such a mess." She covered her face with her hands, then ran her hands through her hair as Sean walked to the other side of the car.

"There can't be two of us running around for long," Gabrielle continued as Sean sat down. "Most people know full well I don't have an estranged twin sister. And I don't see her leaving without a fight, not without another body to double."

"We could offer her Chase." Sean turned to Gabrielle with a mischievous glint in his green eyes. He started the car.

Gabrielle maintained a straight face. "We can't offer her Chase."

"I know, I know." Sean sighed. "That would be wrong."

"Well, I mean there's that, but mostly I'm thinking she wouldn't want him." She smirked.

Sean laughed.

Sean washed dishes in the kitchen. Gabrielle rinsed and placed them into a rack by the sink. As she put a clean glass on a towel beside the rack, someone knocked on the front door of the apartment. Sean looked at her, raising an eyebrow. She bit her lip and walked to the door, peering out through the peephole.

Gabrielle returned to the kitchen, eyes wide.

"It's him," she whispered.

"Mason?" Sean mouthed as he dried his hands on a hand towel. Gabrielle nodded.

"I'm not even here." He left the kitchen.

Mason knocked again.

"Just a minute!" Gabrielle called. She watched, helpless, as Sean walked into his room and shut the door without another word. Then she took a deep breath, returned to the living room, and opened the door. "Um, come in?"

Mason looked back over his shoulder before removing his baseball cap and sunglasses. He stepped into the apartment. "I'm sure it seems rather dodgy that I tracked you down, but you left me in a bit of a bind. I had no idea how to manage your sister after that. Just told her I wasn't feeling well, and that I wanted to rest after we shot our scene. Surprised she didn't ask to join me. Not like there'd be any rest with her around."

Gabrielle felt a surprising pang of jealousy at his words. She pushed the feeling aside as she gestured at the couch. "Would you like to sit down?"

Mason sat on one end of the futon. Gabrielle stood for a moment, torn between sitting next to him on the futon or across from him in the armchair. She settled on the armchair, pressing her lips together as she considered her next words.

"I was wrong before."

Gabrielle looked at Mason with a quizzical tilt to her head.

"You don't look just like her after all," he said.

Gabrielle remembered the way the doppelgänger appeared almost luminous, her blue eyes brighter somehow, her hair shiny and perfectly coiffed. Less frazzled coed, more Parisian model. She looked down at the floor.

"I mean, the facial features are more or less the same, but you're...I don't know, softer somehow," Mason continued. "More, well...human." He said it like a compliment. His words also veered dangerously close to nailing the truth about the doppelgänger. Gabrielle returned his gaze, but only for a moment before looking back down at the carpet.

"The kiss was softer, too."

Gabrielle's eyes widened.

"I'm sorry. That was inappropriate of me."

Sean cleared his throat in the next room. Mason turned to the bedroom door with a look of surprise. He started to stand. "And you already have company. Maybe this was a mistake."

"No, no. It's just my roommate, Sean."

"Oh, right." Mason sat back down. "I'd heard you two were roommates before, but then you weren't. I guess this sister business has been complicating more than just your work."

Gabrielle laughed. "You don't know the half of it."

"Is she...dangerous?" Mason's brows furrowed. "Like, just how serious is the situation? And do the authorities know about this?"

Gabrielle avoided his questions. "How serious are things between you? I mean, it's only been a couple weeks, right?"

"That's the thing. It's all been rather rushed. The only reason my publicist and agent are even cool with our relationship, or whatever it is, is all the extra press it's been getting me. But they expect me to break things off when filming wraps next week. I need to maintain an aura of eligibility for the fans and all of that rubbish."

Mason leaned back on the futon. Gabrielle felt her gaze drawn to his lips. She fought the sudden urge to sit next to him. She sat across from him on the chair instead.

"You make it sound like it's all just a publicity stunt." Gabrielle stared down at the floor. Her voice softened. "Do you like her?" She forced herself to look back up, but Mason looked away as he considered the question.

"I dunno," he said after a few moments. "I mean, I liked the attention, at first. And obviously I think she's beautiful." He looked back with a sly smile. "Smart, too. Funny." His smile faded. "But she's just...she can be too much, you know? Like I can never catch my breath long enough when I'm with her to think things through."

Gabrielle nodded with what she hoped was a look of sympathy even though that annoying pang of jealousy had returned.

Mason continued. "Even off camera it all feels a bit...rehearsed. And I know what people have been saying about us, that she's just using me to get ahead in the business. But it's confusing to them because she's never been like that before. I guess because *you're* not like that." Mason's frown deepened. "How is it nobody but Sean seems to know you have a twin sister, and that she's taking over your life?"

Gabrielle wished she could tell him the truth, but how could she possibly explain getting single white female'd by who knows what from who knows where?

He would think she was insane.

Gabrielle sighed. "Like I said, it's complicated. I can't really go into detail about the specifics." Mason leaned forward, reaching for her hand. She stared down at his fingers wrapped around hers, startled by the intimate gesture as she struggled to think of a rationale. Her heart pounded in her chest. "We didn't grow up together, and I never talked about her, so people assumed I was an only child." It wasn't a lie, not really. "I just want to wait until filming ends before I confront her and she causes any more damage to my career."

"Seems like you'd want her out of the picture sooner rather than later." Mason raised an eyebrow as he let go of her hand.

"Well, the director seems to want her in the literal picture, so I'd rather not spoil his shoot." Gabrielle shrugged. "I know she doesn't want to blow it, either, so at least I've got that going for me."

Mason rose. "I'll do what I can to end things with your sister sooner rather than later...hopefully without making her suspicious. I don't want to cause any more problems for you."

"I'm really sorry you got caught up in my chaos." Gabrielle walked with him to the door. She opened it for him.

Mason stood with his hand against the doorframe as he grinned at her. "Chaos comes with the job. Listen..." He paused, running his free hand through his hair. "I don't want to add to your own chaos, but I'd like to see you again. Unless you think I'm a 'sammie' short of a picnic..."

Gabrielle gave him a shy smile. "I think I'm feeling a sammy short of a picnic myself. I'd like that." She closed the door behind him and leaned against it, sliding down until she sat on the floor.

Sean walked out of his room, grinning. "She may have stolen your life, but you're stealing her man."

Gabrielle rolled her eyes, laughing. "How long did you spend workshopping that tagline?"

"The whole time I was in there."

"Oof."

thirteen

LOUD KNOCKING on the front door of the apartment the next morning woke Gabrielle from a nightmare of small biting things and strange glowing faces in the dark. She was about to walk out of her room when Sean waved her back in, holding a finger to his lips. She watched as he crept to the front door in just his boxers and a rumpled t-shirt. She ducked back into her room, careful not to make a sound.

"Hi," Gabrielle heard him say. "A couple of agents already talked to me the other week. I don't remember their names, but one had a buzz cut and the other one had a mustache." Sean paused, listening. Gabrielle tried to make out what the other person or people were saying but heard only muffled voices. "...Oh, huh. That's weird." Another pause. "Well, like I told them, she moved out last week. Dunno where she's staying now. Wish I could be of more help."

Gabrielle heard the door close. She waited a few moments before walking out to join Sean. He sat on the futon, rubbing his temples. "This is getting serious." He looked up at her, his forehead wrinkling.

"Was it the Feds again?"

"Oh, it was the Feds," Sean said, "but the 'again' part might be up for debate."

Gabrielle raised an eyebrow.

"Agents Miller and Wilson, who speak much more slowly and softly but are no less terrifying than the other guys, said they had no record of anyone speaking to me last week. I'm supposed to give you this card to contact them, but they're bound to show up at the campus or your work sooner or later if they haven't already tracked down your doppelgänger's place."

"But if it wasn't the Feds before, who was it?" Gabrielle frowned.

Sean shrugged. "Who knows?"

Though the day was warm and sunny, the visit from the Federal agents cast a shadow over the rest of the morning. Gabrielle hugged her hoodie to herself as she walked to the lecture hall for her film history class. To her surprise, a couple of people in suits and glasses were waiting outside the double doors. One was a tall black man, the other a shorter white woman with a blunt brown bob. Both wore sunglasses and stern unreadable expressions. Students passed them with curious stares as they walked into the building.

"Gabrielle Johnson?" the man asked, holding up a badge.

Gabrielle nodded, her ears burning. Out of the corner of her eye, she saw Monica pass her. The blonde turned to stare before striding into the building, her expression unreadable.

"I'm Agent Morris and this is Agent Wilson." The man gestured to his partner.

"We just have some questions to ask you," said the woman. "Would you like to ride with us down to the station?"

"I'm supposed to be in class. I can't really afford any more absences," Gabrielle said, but she was flanked on either side by the agents. She had no choice but to follow them to the parking lot and climb into the back seat of an unmarked vehicle.

· · ·

Few people looked up from their paperwork or conversations as the agents led Gabrielle into the station. She followed them into what she assumed was an interrogation room, wondering if she should ask to speak to a lawyer.

"You're a hard lady to find," Agent Morris said, pulling out a seat for Gabrielle.

Huh. Seems like two Gabrielles running around should make me easier to find. Out loud Gabrielle said, "I've been really busy with school and the movie and stuff. Have you been to the set?"

The agents ignored her question, sitting across from her. "Do you know this woman?" Agent Wilson held up a picture. Agent Morris pulled out a pen and notepad, preparing to write.

"That's Simone Weaver. She writes self-help books. My mom made me go with her to a book signing - in Syracuse." Gabrielle figured the more truthfully that she answered their questions, the less suspicious she would appear.

"And that's the only time you saw her?" Agent Morris looked up from his notepad to ask Gabrielle.

Was this a test?

"No," Gabrielle answered. "My mom requested a private consultation or whatever. Simone Weaver asked me to meet her at her hotel room in the Hilton the next day. At, like...three. In the afternoon. I mean, obviously it was afternoon. Who arranges a meeting at three in the morning?"

Gabrielle realized she was starting to babble but could not stop herself. The way they were staring at her made her so nervous, it was worse than being dressed down by Chase.

"Do you recall the date?" Agent Wilson exchanged a glance with Agent Morris.

"It was the first Sunday of spring break. What was that, the sixteenth or the seventeenth? The hotel has it on record. I had to sign in." *But, of course, you already knew that. It's why I'm here.* Gabrielle shifted in her chair.

"And according to their records, you're the last person to see

Simone Weaver. Her room was cleared out, but she never arrived at her next book signing." Agent Wilson peered at Gabrielle.

"I don't know anything about that," she said. "I just went to the meeting to get my mom off my back."

"I see." Agent Wilson rose.

"If you can think of anything else, you know where to reach us." Agent Morris handed Gabrielle a card identical to the one they'd given Sean.

The agents dropped her off back at school. "I wouldn't plan on leaving town any time soon," Agent Wilson said, holding the passenger door open for Gabrielle.

Gabrielle could only nod...

She filled Sean in on her encounter with the federal agents as he drove home. "This is starting to get serious, and I'm still no closer at finding out what to do about the doppelgänger."

"Maybe you need a night off." Sean glanced at her. "I know you're used to managing chaos, and you're not exactly in a position to put your life on hold, but this is a bit much." He paused, thinking. "You don't have any place you need to be tomorrow, right?"

Gabrielle sighed. "I need to finish the rough draft of my research paper, but I can do that at home."

"I'm not scheduled to work wardrobe again until Friday morning, so why don't I take you to the Loft?" Sean's eyes lit up. "You can meet Lance."

"The Loft?" Gabrielle frowned. "What if the FBI's following me?"

"They warned you not to leave town. They didn't say you had to stay home."

Gabrielle remained unconvinced. "But how do you know we won't run into *her*? Have you ever seen her there?"

Sean shrugged. "It's possible, but I doubt it. I know she apparently went wild over spring break, but she seems to be behaving herself during filming. That, or she's spending all her free time with Mason."

Gabrielle's frown deepened, not just from another unwelcome pang of jealousy, but from something else that tugged at her memory. "Oh!" She turned to Sean when she remembered. "Mason said he was going to try to end things, remember?"

"Then she definitely won't be at the Loft," Sean decided.

"She doesn't seem like the sort who would stay in to mope," Gabrielle said.

"No," Sean agreed. "But I think a meat market like the bars on Main would be more her speed. The Loft is too chill for that. C'mon," he pleaded. "Let me take you out. You didn't get to have any fun during spring break. And I really want you to meet Lance."

"Fine," Gabrielle relented.

* * *

Gabrielle regretted her decision as soon as Sean led her into the dimly lit lounge. Low music played on the sound system to allow for conversation. She expected to see her doppelgänger in every intimate leather booth along the outer perimeter, draped over some random guy, a big beefcake like Brandon, or maybe someone shorter but lean and athletic like Mason.

...or maybe even Mason himself.

Gabrielle cringed at the thought. Just because he planned to break things off sooner rather than later did not mean he really meant it. Besides, her doppelgänger could be really persuasive.

"There he is," Sean said.

"Mason?" Gabrielle looked around.

Sean laughed. "No, Lance." He put his hands on the sides of Gabrielle's arms and turned her to face someone manning the end of the bar. The purple lighting of the bar highlighted the man's tufts of blond hair as he bent over to scoop ice into a glass.

Gabrielle smoothed the sleeves of the silky aquamarine shirt she wore with black pants and flats, looking like she'd just got off work from one of the nearby offices. She followed Sean past people dressed in everything from casual but trendy to elegant clothing to business attire. They sat in small groups on leather chairs and sofas arranged around small coffee tables. Most did not glance up from their animated conversations.

Sean was dressed more casually than Gabrielle in a black shirt and dark jeans, and he still looked like a million bucks. But even his good looks were no match for Lance's fine features and flawless skin. Good genes alone could not account for his apparent lack of pores. Gabrielle realized she was staring. She looked down to admire the glimmering flecks of gold and silver that accented the black countertop.

If Lance noticed anything weird about her behavior, he played it off, setting cocktail napkins down in front of Gabrielle and Sean. Sean had probably warned him that she could be a bit awkward. Hopefully he attributed the staring to that.

"Hey, you," he said to Sean, his voice warm, intimate even. He turned to Gabrielle and held out his hand. "I'm Lance. Sean's told me all about you."

Gabrielle's eyes flitted to his face as she accepted his hand. She felt a jolt of recognition as he gave her hand a light squeeze in a brief handshake. "Same. I mean, Sean's told me a lot about you, too." Her hand returned to her lap and her eyes returned to the counter.

"She doesn't get out very much," Sean teased.

"So, what's the special occasion?" Lance began mixing a drink as he talked, even though they had yet to order anything. "Is Hump Day even a thing in your line of work?"

"Seriously." Sean laughed. "Nah, Bri just had kind of a rough day. The you-know-who caught up with her at school today."

"Sounds like you've been having a lot of rough days lately," Lance said to Gabrielle. "What are you drinking?"

"Oh." She'd been so preoccupied that she forgot to think about her order. Gabrielle glanced down at the list of craft cocktails Lance set in front of her. "The lavender one sounds interesting."

Gabrielle found that she could not look at Lance for long. Something about his high cheekbones and those strange amber eyes, an almost impossible shade of golden brown. It wasn't just how handsome he was. She felt like she was tumbling into an uncanny valley as she sipped her drink and listened to Sean and Lance talk.

The drink did not help, to be honest. It tasted amazing, sure, but there was something familiar about the floral notes. Then she remembered. Simone's chamomile tea.

Sean excused himself to the restroom.

Gabrielle looked up from her drink to Lance's bemused expression, then back down at her drink. He wasn't...he wouldn't try anything here, would he? It was just a coincidence. The lavender wasn't what drugged her. It was something else.

"I'm sorry. Have we met?"

Though Lance's tone was light, Gabrielle responded seriously. "Haven't we?" She tilted her head as she wondered what poor soul's life he had stolen. Was the real Lance that beautiful, or had he taken liberties with his appearance just as her doppelgänger had with hers?

Taken aback, Lance busied himself with cleaning glasses behind the counter. "It's not how it looks," he said. "I'm not like her. She isn't..." He paused, considering his words." She isn't *authorized* to be here. That's why she needs..." He stopped.

"Needs what?" Gabrielle asked, bewildered. Everything he said left her with more questions than answers.

What did he mean by authorized?

Authorized by who?

Or what...

"I can't say any more than that, I'm sorry. The less you know, the better. But trust me when I say some of us are working on setting things right." Lance looked sincere. "Please don't say anything to Sean." His strange amber eyes were pleading.

Gabrielle found herself nodding despite her unease. She felt a growing suspicion she was mixed up in something bigger than her problem with the doppelgänger, and that problem already felt too big to wrap her brain around.

"You guys getting to know each other?" Sean sat back down in his chair, grinning at Lance and Gabrielle.

She pasted a placid expression onto her face. . "Yeah, I was just asking Lance about his intentions."

Lance met her eyes with a look of understanding, even a hint of respect. She wasn't ready to say anything to Sean, but she wanted Lance to know he wasn't off the hook, either.

"His intentions? Good grief, Bri, it's only been a couple weeks." Sean gave her shoulder an affectionate squeeze. "We can be a little protective of each other," he told Lance.

Lance's lips curved into a smile. "I've picked up on that."

* * *

Gabrielle was quiet as Sean drove home. "So, what do you think?" he asked.

"I'm too tired to think," Gabrielle said. "It's been a long day."

"I meant about Lance," Sean pressed.

"Oh. He's something else. I can see why you like him." She leaned back in the seat, closing her eyes in feigned sleepiness.

By the time she undressed for bed and crawled under the covers, Gabrielle was wide awake. She stared at the ceiling, turning the events of the day over and over in her mind. Her exchange with Lance had left her feeling even more on edge than getting grilled by the federal agents at school did.

And in between all that, thoughts of Mason slipped in. Of words both spoken and unspoken and even more interesting thoughts than that. At last, she slipped into a deep sleep.

fourteen

"CUT!" the assistant director called.

Mason untangled himself from Gabrielle's strange sister and sat up, his white shirt partly unbuttoned and pulled out of his jeans. Her character had pushed him back onto an opulent king-sized bed, the velvety plum comforter as rumpled as his shirt.

"One more time for safety?" Gabrielle's sister grinned at Mason, running a hand down his back. She wore a skimpy green dress, one strap sliding precariously off her shoulder, and stilettos.

Mason tried not to recoil at her touch. He had grown more and more uncomfortable in her presence since learning the truth. Well, some of the truth.

A little?

It occurred to him that the real Gabrielle had never even told him her sister's real name. He decided it was probably safer that way, lest he call the imposter her real name by mistake. On set, they used character names. In private was another story.

He looked up as Harlow Hansen approached the bed. "That last take was perfect. I think we got everything we needed from this scene."

"Oh. Okay." Gabrielle's sister forced a smile, but Mason could sense her disappointment by the way she tightened her jaw.

"We're moving on to Annelise's scene in the hall when she sees Zack with Victoria and gets the wrong idea. So you're done for today," Harlow told Mason. The film crew began removing equipment from the bedroom of the gated estate they'd rented for the shoot. "Tomorrow we're shooting the big confrontation between you and Annalise, early. Then you have the rest of the day and all of the weekend off."

"What about me?" Gabrielle's sister looked at Harlow, the barest hint of a pout pulling down the corners of her lips.

Harlow looked down at his call sheet. "I don't think we need Victoria on set again until next week some time, but you can double check with Chase."

The woman's slight pout deepened into a full-on frown. Harlow did not notice. He was already walking away.

"Welp, I guess that's it for today." Mason pushed himself off the bed. He began to adjust his clothing as if he would not be removing everything in the wardrobe department a few minutes from now.

Mason pretended not to notice as Gabrielle's sister watched him leave the room. She caught up with him in the spacious hallway outside the bedroom and wrapped her arms around one of his. "So, what are we doing this weekend?" She nuzzled his neck. In heels, she almost matched him in height, which had led to a lot of changing between heels and flats during filming depending on the shooting angle.

"Hi, guys!" Natalia Martinez walked into the hallway. Like Mason, the actress was starring in her first feature film. Just as he'd gotten his start on a soap opera in New Zealand, she'd achieved a small degree of fame. The telenovela she starred in had begun to attract a big international audience. *A New Man* was intended to be a breakthrough romantic comedy hit for both of them.

Instead of a saucy dress and the long bouncy curls that defined her look as Emmanuella on the show of the same name, Natalia wore a modest pink blouse and khaki pants. She was playing Maria, Zack's forgotten best friend with a here-to-fore unrequited crush. A dark messy braid cascaded down her back, and glasses completed the look. She was, of course, still gorgeous, with her dimpled cheeks and big brown eyes, and about as mousy as a jungle cat, but that was Hollywood for you.

Right now, Natalia's beautiful brown eyes sparkled as she said, "Settle down, you two. From some of the dailies I've seen, we'll be lucky to keep this movie PG-13."

"Don't worry. I'm sure you and Mason have really good chemistry, too," Gabrielle's sister said with a sly smile. She held onto Mason's arm a little tighter.

"I'm not worried," Natalia said, returning her grin, one eyebrow arched in amusement. She turned to Mason. "Are you going to Tiffany Sharp's party tomorrow night? She rented a place on the Canadian side because she has a show here in Buffalo, and then she starts the Canadian leg of her tour. I'm seeing her in Toronto on Saturday."

"I don't think I got an invite," Mason said. He remembered the name of the singer who had a cameo in the house party scene they shot last week as part of the band, but she had been a bright blur of sequins and long blond waves. They hadn't spoken.

"She can be particular about who she invites." Natalia cast a side-long glance at Gabrielle's sister. "But I can vouch for you. I'll text you the details." Natalia touched Mason's free arm as she passed them in the hall. "See you tomorrow morning."

Gabrielle's sister watched her go. Then she turned to Mason. "I want to go to a party."

"I don't know," he said, shrugging her off. He continued walking down the hall to an elegant spiral staircase leading downstairs. "I'm feeling pretty knackered."

"Okay," Gabrielle's sister said. She followed him down the stairs, undeterred. "Let's stay in. Your place. We can get room service," she purred into his ear when they reached the bottom.

Mason turned to face her. "I'm sorry, but I think I need some time to myself this weekend," he said, tucking a strand of red hair behind her ear to soften the blow of his words. "It's been a long week." He walked to the room that had been designated as his dressing room, feeling her eyes on his back the whole way.

A bleary-eyed Gabrielle stared at the screen of her laptop. Five pages down, five to go. At least she was finally making progress on her research paper again. She considered rewatching one of the movies she was including in her essay but thought better of it.

She was likely to doze off, and monsters and mayhem were not the sort of film content she wanted informing her dreams.

Gabrielle hadn't slept well last night as it was. She awoke that morning in a tangle of sweaty sheets, hitting snooze several times before she finally crawled out of her bed. Already her dreams were fading from memory, but she knew Mason had been in one of the better ones. Until it segued into a strangely-hued nightmare of alien landscapes and monsters with glowing eyes and sharp fangs.

Gabrielle was contemplating a nap when her new phone began to vibrate beside her right hand. She reached for it, expecting it to be Sean or her parents. Nobody else had her new number yet. She did not recognize the number, but Gabrielle answered anyway. "Hello?"

"Hi, Gabrielle? Or do you prefer Bri? I'm sorry. I never thought to ask before, but Sean calls you Bri, so Bri it is. Unless you prefer Gabrielle. And now he's looking at me like I've gone mental. It's Mason, by the way."

Gabrielle laughed. "Bri's fine," she said. "Hi, Mason."

"Right, so there's this party tomorrow night. It's being hosted by this singer. Tiffany Sharp? I don't know if you've heard of her, but she rented a place on the Canadian side, and I was wondering if you'd like to go with me. To the party?"

Gabrielle was silent. She didn't listen to the radio a lot, but

Tiffany Sharp's music and image had been inescapable. Also, it was Mason. Asking her on a date. It was a date, right?

"Hum, Bri?" Mason's worried voice came over the line.

"What?" Gabrielle snapped back to reality. "Oh, sorry. Just had an out-of-body experience for a moment there."

"So, you're a fan?"

"I...I'm not *not* a fan." The truth was that although Gabrielle had some idea of who Tiffany Sharp was and what her music sounded like, she couldn't name a single song.

Whatever. It's not like there's going to be a pop quiz.

Heh. Pop.

Aloud, Gabrielle said, "I'd love to go." She probably wouldn't even get a chance to meet her hostess, but maybe she should research her music just in case.

"Great." Gabrielle was surprised at the relief in Mason's voice. "Her show ends at ten, and the party starts at eleven or so, so I guess I'll pick you up around ten-thirty? Or maybe we should grab a bite to eat first. We should probably eat."

"Up to you," Gabrielle said, bewildered. She was usually eyeing the exits at eleven, not making her entrance. Someone was speaking to Mason, Sean from the sounds of it. Gabrielle rolled her eyes, shaking her head. She waited for Mason to come back on the line.

"Your roommate has informed me eight is a more reasonable hour to pick up a date, so dinner first, and we'll play it by ear after that," Mason said.

"Sounds great!"

Gabrielle could not stop grinning after they ended the call, glad she'd been able to replace her enhanced license to travel across the border without too much trouble. She looked online for a playlist of Tiffany Sharp's frothy shimmering music and fell back in her bed, sinking into the pillows.

A few moments later, she bolted upright.

"Oh, no!"

· · ·

"I have to cancel my date with Mason," Gabrielle told Sean when he came home. "Those federal agents pretty much told me not to leave town, let alone the country!"

"Yeah, about that." Sean sat down beside Gabrielle on her bed. He tugged away the pillow she clutched to her chest, handing her his unlocked phone. "Check out the headline."

Gabrielle read, her eyes growing wide.

Missing Influencer Spotted in Cancun Resort, Publishers Livid.

Gabrielle clicked on the headline to see the full article. As she scanned the story, she saw a few grainy photos of a blond woman in designer sunglasses lounging by a swimming pool. In the last photo, the woman removed her glasses. It sure looked like a photo of Simone Weaver. But the real Simone Weaver was long gone. She had to be.

Right?

"Is this for real?" Gabrielle turned to Sean.

"Real enough to let you off the hook."

"But how can this-"

Gabrielle's confusion faded as her conversation with Lance last night came back to her. Something about others working to set things right. Someone must have disguised themselves as the missing author. If only they would do something about the culprit behind the real Simone's disappearance however many years before. Somehow, she doubted *that* Simone was living her best life in Cancun.

Another memory came back to Gabrielle, one of being fed on by horrible creatures in another world. Had the real Simone died of the gruesome fate Lance had rescued Gabrielle from?

"Hey." Sean nudged Gabrielle with his shoulder. "This is a good thing. You're no longer a person of interest, and you're free to go on a date with the man of your dreams." He grinned. "Maybe even my dreams, if I didn't already have Lance."

Gabrielle returned his smile, but the feeling of unease remained. "Still seems risky. What if my doppelgänger finds out?"

Sean shrugged. "Talk Mason into eating on the Canadian side. Or maybe go to the Falls. It's so busy, I doubt you'd have to worry about running into each other, even if she did happen to go there."

"I guess I don't have any more excuses." Gabrielle's smile widened.

Sean shook his head. "Your fate is sealed."

fifteen

"YOU KNOW, YOU DON'T 'GIRL' very well," Sean observed from the bed. "You're like the antithesis of Monica. Not that there's anything wrong with that," he added. "That's one of the nice things about Lance. I don't have to wait an extra half hour when we go out just for him to look the same as he did when I arrived."

"I'm just a girl standing in front of a closet asking for something to wear," Gabrielle said. "I couldn't possibly be 'girling' any harder than I am right now."

Sean rose and walked to her closet. He handed Gabrielle a couple things. "Here."

"Jeans and a tank top?" Gabrielle looked at Sean, raising an eyebrow. "I might as well top it off with a denim jacket. Go full Canadian tuxedo."

Sean rolled his eyes. "Those jeans fit you like a glove, and you haven't worn them since...well, you know. And the tank top shows a little skin without looking like you're trying too hard."

"I'm going out on a date to a party being thrown by one of the biggest 'it' girls in Hollywood," Gabrielle said. "I should look like I'm trying a little."

"Trust me." Sean grinned. "I swear, you have the best clavicle."

"Yeah, I get that a lot." Gabrielle made a face as she held up the hangers and regarded her reflection in the mirror. "Will you at least help me with my hair and makeup?"

"Of course," Sean said. "But no 'Extreme Makeovers.' It's you Mason likes, and it's you he's picking up tonight. Go shower." He squeezed her shoulders and left the room.

An hour later Gabrielle sat on the futon in jeans and a dark blue tank top, running her fingers through her still-damp red curls. Sean assured her that his new mousse would help tame her frizzy locks. He conceded to applying a deeper shade of pink lip gloss than Gabrielle normally wore, plus a creamy shimmering eyeshadow, but otherwise she looked more or less the same.

"I think I'm getting stood up," she said to Sean, who sat beside her on the futon with an amused smile on his face as he watched her fret. "He said he'd call or text or whatever when he was on his way, and it's almost eight."

"Never in the history of mankind has someone been less likely to stand someone up for a date," Sean said. Her phone buzzed as if on cue. "Told you so."

Gabrielle rolled her eyes and answered her phone.

"Hey, it's Mason. Bad news."

Gabrielle's face fell. Sean looked at her, his forehead wrinkling in concern.

"Filming ran a bit later than expected, but Harlow assures me we're wrapping up shortly. Natalia's about to claw his face off if she has to squeeze out any more tears." He paused to listen to someone. "No, I'm not just saying that because Latinas are supposed to be feisty," Mason said. "I'd claw his face off myself if I had talons like you." To Gabrielle, he said. "Do you think maybe Sean can drop you off to save time? There's a pub nearby that I'm told has choice burgers."

Gabrielle released the breath she did not realize she had been holding. She turned to Sean with a smile of relief. "He needs you to drop me off. Filming went over."

Gabrielle waved as Sean drove away. Though Mason wanted her to meet him in the foyer of the estate, she decided to wait outside rather than make another attempt at the charade of being the doppelgänger around others. She struggled to act natural as it was just being herself, let alone pretending to be someone else being...herself.

Just thinking about it made Gabrielle's head spin. Mason would be out soon anyway.

Gabrielle leaned against the wrought-iron gate, hugging the leather jacket Sean had loaned her closer to her body. Chilly night. She almost changed her mind about waiting outside when she heard footsteps on the pavement. A tentative smile spread across her face as she turned to look. Her grin faded as Chase stepped through the gate, a lighter and cigarette in hand. She maintained her composure but felt her inner self shrink under his withering glare as he walked over.

"I'd ask what you're doing here when your name wasn't even on the call sheet, but I guess you're waiting for Mason. How long until you drop him for Harlow or the director?"

"I should go." Easier said than done without a vehicle, Gabrielle realized as she backed away from Chase. She found herself wondering if the other Gabrielle had traded her car in for something newer and shinier. She frowned. She really liked that car.

"What's the matter, Bri? Don't like being called out on your game?" Chase sneered as he lit his cigarette. "I always knew there was something off about you," he said after he took a puff, "but I never took you for a fame whore. I guess that's why you turned me down. Too low of a rung on the ladder to success."

Gabrielle's eyes flashed. She turned to walk away without a clear destination in mind but stopped. Instead, she took a step closer to

Chase, whose own eyes widened in surprise. "That is *not* why I turned you down. You're like, way older. You were basically my boss. Asking me out was a total abuse of authority, and you know it." Gabrielle jabbed a finger at his chest. Chase backed away, dropping his cigarette. Gabrielle crushed it under a well-worn slip-on shoe. "And Mason isn't a rung on some stupid metaphorical ladder, either. I like him."

"Enjoy it while you can," Chase said as he walked back through the gate. "Mason has his own ladder to climb. You're not even a rung."

Your face is a rung. Gabrielle rolled her eyes, leaning back against the gate.

"Hey, you!"

Gabrielle looked up as Mason jogged down the walkway and out the gate to meet her. "That ratbag wasn't bothering you, was he? I know he's exchanged a few words with your sister, but she always shrugs him off like water so the only one who comes off looking bad is him."

"I'm okay," Gabrielle said. She felt less self-conscious about her outfit now that Mason stood before her in jeans and a forest green tee shirt. But even dressed casually, Mason still possessed that hard-to-define star quality. It wasn't like her doppelgänger's eerie glow. Some people just shone a little brighter than others.

"There's that sweet smile," Mason said. "Let's go."

Mason pulled his rental car, a sporty black BMW coupe with heated leather seats, into the small parking lot of a nondescript brick restaurant on a quiet corner. "I think this is the place," he said as they walked to the entrance.

The modest exterior was misleading. Inside, the pub was elegant and refined, with lit candles on every dark wooden table and booths on one side with leather cushions. Gabrielle worried they were underdressed, but the hostess, who wore a long-sleeved black velvet dress, smiled warmly at them when she asked if they preferred a table or booth. If she recognized Mason, she did not show it.

"Booth?" Mason asked Gabrielle. She nodded.

The hostess led them to a booth, setting food and cocktail menus down on the table. Gabrielle noted a lavender honey drink with amusement but settled on something with rose syrup and champagne instead. It even came with candied rose petals. As they sipped their drinks and waited for their burgers, Mason told Gabrielle about growing up in New Zealand, and she evaded questions about her own childhood as best she could.

Even if Gabrielle did not have the made-up sister dilemma to contend with, she disliked talking about her past. And it wasn't like anything particularly bad or traumatic had happened to her. Her life simply had never been that interesting, until now anyway - like the universe had waited until the past month to throw all the excitement her way at once.

"So, what is it that made you decide you wanted to work in the film industry?" Mason asked.

"I'm not sure," Gabrielle said. "I've loved watching movies since I was a little kid. When it came time to choose a major for college, I don't know, it seemed like there were so many different ways to get involved, and I just wanted to be a part of it." She considered telling him about her ultimate goal of directing, but the server arrived with their food and she lost her nerve.

Instead, Gabrielle asked Mason about his own start in film and television. He told her about some of his favorite storylines on the soap opera he starred in back home, *Sons of Wellington*, and about a big falling-out he had with one of his co-stars.

"So, then the director gave that bloody muppet a good rark up." Mason paused, narrowing his eyes as he looked at Gabrielle with mock suspicion. "Are you smiling because it's a funny story or because I sound funny when I tell it?"

"Yes," Gabrielle said. Her grin widened.

Mason smiled back. "Anyway, after that whole cock-up, the

network had no choice but to recast his role. The new guy doesn't even have the same eye color and he's several inches shorter, but up until a few years ago, the character was also a little kid."

Gabrielle laughed.

She managed to avoid the topic of her "sister" for the rest of the meal. Mason was so easy to talk to, she almost forgot to be nervous around him. Until his hand brushed against hers as he helped her put her jacket back on. A delicious shiver ran up her spine as she wondered what the rest of the evening would hold.

sixteen

GABRIELLE STOLE sidelong glances at Mason as they drove to the Peace Bridge over the Niagara River. As a child, Gabrielle liked to pretend that the bridge, lit purple at night, led to another world. And tonight, it almost felt like it did. Only this world would just be filled with actors and pop stars instead of evil bloodsucking monsters.

Mason turned to her. "Which lane?"

"What?" Gabrielle blinked away her confusion. "Oh, don't ask me. I always pick wrong. Even if I pick the shortest lane, it always ends up being the one held up by Customs officials." She felt a twinge of nervousness at the prospect herself. What if the FBI still considered her a person of interest?

Her unease grew as Mason picked the shortest lane himself.

"Hey, are you okay?" he asked.

"Yeah," Gabrielle said. "Just a little nervous about the party. I can't remember the last time I went to any house party, let alone one with a bunch of celebrities."

"Aww, we don't bite." Mason reached over to pat her hand.

That's too bad, Gabrielle thought. She bit her lip on a smile, though she was certain her blush gave her inappropriate thoughts away. If Mason noticed, he was too kind to say so.

The line moved at a brisk pace. Gabrielle took out her license when they reached the window. After Mason gave everything to the dispassionate border patrol agent and stated their reason for visiting Canada, the agent looked between Gabrielle and her license.

"State your name and hometown."

"Uhm, Gabrielle Johnson. Buffalo." She hoped he did not notice the tremor in her voice, but his watery gray eyes and craggy face gave nothing away. The agent took one last look at her license, then glanced back at Gabrielle before returning everything to Mason.

"Enjoy your visit." He smiled, waving them forward.

Gabrielle breathed a sigh of relief. Mason looked at her. "Is your sister in trouble with the law in Canada or something?"

"No." Gabrielle laughed. "I guess *everything* makes me nervous."

Mason drove through Fort Erie along the lake until they arrived at the lakefront cottage Tiffany had rented. The expansive front lawn was a fairy wonderland of floodlights that cycled through all the colors of the rainbow. A smattering of cherry and magnolia trees were in full bloom and strung with still more lights, small and flickering like colorful fireflies. Daffodils and pink and purple irises lined the walkway leading up to a yellow two-story cottage with a white wraparound porch and dark tiled roof.

Inside, the cottage buzzed with activity. It had an open floor plan with vaulted ceilings and huge picture windows. Partygoers sat on a couch and leather armchairs arranged around a marble fireplace in the great room. Still more mingled in the dining room or outside around a firepit Gabrielle could see through the windows. A deejay was set up in a corner of the great room, spinning everything from Tiffany's up-tempo pop hits to slower songs that prompted couples to hold each other and sway wherever they found room to dance.

Mason helped Gabrielle out of her jacket and hung it on a coat rack near the front door. A young woman with dimples and long enviable brown curls walked toward him with a grin.

Natalia Martinez, Gabrielle presumed. She wore a white jumpsuit with long sheer sleeves, a bold gamble at a crowded party like this. Though the petite actress could not have been more than five feet tall, she cut a commanding figure as she strode through the crowd. She veered to the side, narrowly avoiding a party foul when someone rose from an armchair and turned around without looking, their glass filled to the brim with dark red wine.

"You made it!" Natalia threw her arms around Mason and squeezed. "Oh," she said when she let go, noticing Gabrielle standing beside him with a shy smile. "You're here, too." Her expression soured. "Oh, there's Tiffany!" She hurried across the room. A woman with a mane of blond waves and curls, in a little black dress that sparkled like the night sky, walked down a narrow spiral staircase.

"I take it we don't get along?" Gabrielle's smile faded.

Mason turned to her with a wry grin. "Not really, no. Your sister gets on well enough with most of the cast and crew, except for maybe Chase, who doesn't get on well with anyone," he continued as he led her to the kitchen, "but she's a bit jealous of Natalia, and there's been some tension between them. Oh, full bar." Mason walked to a large lit cabinet with glass doors. "Do you want anything?"

"I think I'm sticking with soda for now," Gabrielle said. "I don't want to get sloppy at my first big Hollywood party. Sounds like my sister has done enough damage to my professional reputation," she added.

Mason took a couple of sodas out of a fridge stocked full of cold drinks and beer, even some regional craft beers. "You mean with Natalia?" He handed a can to Gabrielle. "You don't have to worry about her."

"Oh, of course not. I mean, it's not like some big movie star could ever have any impact on my future as a dir...err, in the industry,"

Gabrielle stammered. She remembered she still hadn't told Mason about her true aspirations.

"Yeah, nah, Natalia's not the sort to hold a grudge." Mason walked to the unoccupied breakfast nook in the corner of the kitchen area, resting one of his arms on the back cushion. After a moment, Gabrielle sat down beside him. She felt very aware of his arm draped over the cushion behind her, though he wasn't touching her. "So..."

"So..." Gabrielle repeated.

They looked at each other and laughed.

"I don't remember if I told you earlier, but you look amazing," Mason said.

Gabrielle felt her cheeks grow warm from his appreciative gaze. "To be honest, I feel a little underdressed compared to Natalia and our sparkly hostess," she said.

"Are you? I hadn't noticed," Mason said, still looking into her eyes with a funny little smile on his face.

Gabrielle's blush deepened, but she returned his smile.

"Hey, Mason, just the guy I wanted to see." A tall lanky man with spiky black hair and a lopsided grin approached them. "You don't mind if I steal your man for a bit, do you?" he asked Gabrielle.

My man?

Oh. He thinks I'm the me that isn't me. Must be part of the cast.

Mason gave Gabrielle a look of apology as she stood. "It's fine," she said. "Maybe I'll go...I dunno, find Natalia, or something."

"You sure?" Mason's brow furrowed.

"Yeah, we'll catch up later." Gabrielle offered a reassuring grin.

Gabrielle decided she could use some fresh air, so she walked out the back patio doors. A cool lake breeze chilled the night air, but she noticed someone with long brown curls nursing a glass of rosé in a chair near the firepit. The chair beside her was unoccupied. Gabrielle bit her upper lip, considering. Then she walked to the chair and sat down. Natalia turned to her with a look of skepticism, waiting for her to speak.

"I know I haven't exactly made the best first impression. If I ever stuck my foot in my mouth or said or did something that I shouldn't have, I'm really sorry. This is all just so new to me. The movie. Mason. All of it," Gabrielle said truthfully. "And you're so pretty and intimidating and..." she trailed off.

Gabrielle worried she sounded like a babbling idiot, but Natalia's expression had softened.

"Look, I get it," she said, setting her glass down on a side table. "Starting out in this business can be tough. That's why it's important to surround yourself with good people. And Mason?" She caught his eye through the glass doors to the house, and he waved. Natalia turned back to Gabrielle. "He's good people. I hope you are, too." Though her words were serious, her eyes were kind. She rose to warm her hands over the firepit.

"I try to be," Gabrielle said, joining her.

Natalia gave her a considering look. "People say you're just using him to get ahead, but watching the two of you here, it seems like you really do like him."

"Do you want to know a secret?" Gabrielle said. "I don't even want to be an actress. I feel a lot more comfortable behind the camera." Before she could say anything more, someone came up behind them and wrapped strong but slender arms around their shoulders.

"Natalia, you're here!" Tiffany planted a noisy kiss on the actress's cheek and turned to Gabrielle. "You're new," she said, her blue eyes sparkling as brightly as her dress.

"I talked to you earlier," Natalia said, untangling herself from the singer. "What have you been smoking?"

"Nothing, I swear!" Tiffany giggled. "I don't even drink when I'm on tour. Tony – that's my manager," she explained to Gabrielle, "he did tell me to lay off the energy drinks, though. Says they make me goofy. Do I seem goofy to you? Don't answer that." She sat down in the chair Natalia vacated and patted the arm of the chair beside her. "I want to talk about you instead. Tell me everything there is to know about you."

Gabrielle turned to Natalia for help, but an amused smile spread across the actress's face. "You heard the lady," Natalia said. "I could use another glass of wine." She turned to go, and Gabrielle realized she was on her own.

"We haven't been introduced already, have we?" Tiffany's blue eyes widened with concern. "Because if we have, I'm so sorry I forgot your name. I get a little loopy from all the traveling and performing and stuff. I had to do, like, three shows in New York City last week because the club kept selling out. Tony thinks I can easily draw the audience for a big stadium tour next time, but...I dunno. I like performing at clubs. Feels more...intimate, you know?"

"I guess so?" Gabrielle had no idea what she should say. "I don't know a lot about the music industry. I work in film."

"Oh, that's right," Tiffany said, even though she could not have possibly known that. She sat back in her chair. Then she slapped her forehead before turning back to Gabrielle. "Please don't hate me, but I totally forgot your name."

"Gabrielle, but I..."

"God, I love your hair. It's just so...red!"

Any fears Gabrielle had about Tiffany grilling her faded as it became apparent how easy it was to keep the singer talking about anything else. So far, she'd learned that Tiffany had been named after her mom's favorite pop star as a child (which Gabrielle agreed was, like, totally ironic), her star sign was Gemini with a Libra rising and moon in Virgo, whatever that meant, and she had her big break on an ensemble teen variety show. She met Natalia when the telenovela actress appeared as a special guest on her show. Now Tiffany was the one with a cameo in Natalia and Mason's movie. And Tiffany learned

Gabrielle was a film student with a small role in the same movie, and that she sometimes worked as a production assistant.

Gabrielle could not even take offense to what others might interpret as a lack of interest. The singer was so warm and friendly, it would be like getting mad at an overenthusiastic golden retriever. Only Gabrielle was pretty confident she did not have to worry about Tiffany Sharp piddling on her shoe. So, bonus.

"Hey, if you're done chatting Gabrielle's ear off, I think her date misses her," Natalia said to Tiffany as she came back outside with Mason in tow.

He wore an apologetic smile as he reached for Gabrielle's hand, and she rose from the chair. "Sorry," he said. "My publicist called when I was in the middle of talking to Dan. She usually doesn't bother me with business on a Friday night, but she booked me for this interview, and it's kind of a big deal. So I have to fly to New York City tomorrow morning. My flight doesn't leave until eleven or so, but..." Mason frowned.

"We need to go?"

"Yeah." Mason turned to Tiffany, forcing a smile. "It's been a real cracker of a party. I wish we could stay longer."

Tiffany stood up and wrapped a protective arm around Gabrielle's shoulder, pulling her in close as she glared at Mason. "You better take good care of my girl Gabriella," she said. "We're practically besties. Don't you dare hurt her."

"He won't." Natalia untangled Tiffany from Gabrielle. "Drive safe. I'll see you next week," she told Mason.

seventeen

"DAMN. I would have been a lot more protective of my time with you had I known it would be cut short," Mason said as he drove away from the cottage. "I thought we had the whole weekend ahead of us."

Gabrielle felt a tingling jolt of excitement at the thought of Mason wanting to spend the whole weekend with her, followed by disappointment that he had to go to New York City instead. For the last few hours, she had forgotten all about her doppelgänger and all the other complications that stood between her and Mason, including his career - up until the moment it spoiled their first date.

Assuming there would be a second...

Gabrielle stared out the window, chewing on this possibility.

"So, what did you think of your first big Hollywood party?" Mason asked. He touched Gabrielle's knee with his hand, and she almost jumped out of her skin.

"It was...nice," she said.

"Just nice?"

"Very nice," Gabrielle said. "Honestly, it didn't strike me as all that different from any other party I've been to." *Except nobody ignored me at this one.* "I don't want to use the word 'mundane,' especially for that cottage, which was absolutely amazing, but...I dunno, it all seemed pretty normal. Relatively speaking."

Maybe *normal* wasn't the right word for someone like Tiffany Sharp in particular, but she was pretty down to earth for a pop star... in her own spacy way.

"They aren't all like that," Mason said, "but Tiffany is very particular about who she invites to her parties or allows into her circle. I know she seems a bit, well, thick, but Natalia tells me she's actually pretty smart about the business. You just need to catch her in the quieter moments."

Sounds like a good resource, Gabrielle almost caught herself saying to Mason. It sounded like something her mother would say. Instead, she liked to think of Tiffany as a...well, maybe "friend" was too strong of a word, even if the singer did say they were practically besties, but she was definitely "good people," as Natalia would say. Tiffany could teach Simone Weaver a thing or two about performance and authenticity that was for sure. There were limits to the fake Gabrielle's business acumen, like her ability to play nice with others.

"You got quiet," Mason said as they neared the border. Once again, he selected the shortest lane. This time, they were less fortunate as the lane came to a halt.

"On the bright side," Gabrielle said as additional agents appeared to examine the contents of a van a few cars ahead of them in line, "we get to spend more time together before you take me home." She turned to Mason and smiled.

Mason returned her grin. "Yeah, well, as cozy as this car is, it's less than ideal for continuing our date. Plus, someone keeps staring at me from the other lane. I wonder if she's a fan." He winked.

Gabrielle leaned forward to look past Mason at the other vehicle. A little girl stared unabashedly from the backseat, clutching a teddy bear to her chest. "Just a kid being a kid, I think." She laughed.

The lane started moving again, and they made it through the gate without incident. Mason grew silent as they passed over the

Peace Bridge. Gabrielle gazed at him, admiring the line of his jaw, and his lips, which appeared almost pursed as he puzzled something out. "Now you're the one who's quiet," she said.

Mason surprised her by pulling off to the side of the road. "Bugger." He turned to Gabrielle. "I know it's late, and it's wildly inappropriate of me to ask, but do you want to come over? Just to hang out," he added, holding up his hands.

Gabrielle surprised herself by saying, "Yes."

Mason sighed with relief as he pulled into the parking lot of his hotel. "No sign of any photographers," he said. "Must have given up for the night." He turned to Gabrielle. "They're mostly here for Natalia. She has a suite across the hall from mine, and the bigger fan base, but I'd hate to chance us being found out by your sister."

"That would be bad." Gabrielle's eyes widened at the prospect. She knew she was pressing her luck, but when Mason opened the door and held out his hand, she pushed aside her reservations to take it.

The hotel was quiet as they took the elevator and walked down the hall to Mason's corner suite. "Oh, wow," Gabrielle said as he let her into the room. She hung up her jacket and walked across the marble floor to sit on a brown leather couch. The room was painted in muted colors, with gold-framed artwork and tall potted plants.

"You think this is nice, you should see Natalia's room." Mason sat down beside her. "She has the presidential suite. It's huge, with this two-person tub, a heated toilet seat in the loo. I mean, not that we... she and I, we're just friends. I've never stayed there. She just had to show it off because, I mean, *heated* toilet seat."

Gabrielle laughed. "Does that mean yours isn't heated? Maybe I should go." She feigned a disappointed frown as she started to rise from the couch. Mason reached for her hand.

"I have a walk-in shower that's pretty nice," he said with a straight face as he gazed up at her. "It's no heated toilet seat, but it's way better than some stupid two-person tub."

"I'll keep that in mind." Gabrielle sat back down, still admiring the room. "I've been to the rooftop bar once, but I never saw any of the rooms. This is nice."

"The gig has its perks," Mason said. He reached for a remote on the ornate coffee table in front of the couch. "Movie?"

They settled on a romantic comedy both had seen. "This way we won't miss anything if we get distracted," Mason said. He made her laugh, pointing out ways *A New Man* would deviate from the film on the screen. "You see, she has a ponytail, but Natalia's character wears her hair in a braid, which is totally different, but, you know, still ugly."

"Totally," Gabrielle agreed, mimicking his scholarly expression.

"But once she lets her hair down, she gets to be the ingenue." Mason looked away from the screen to consider Gabrielle. "Now, yours is too short for a ponytail or a braid, but it's red and it's wild so we know that you're a villain." He leaned toward her, tucking a strand behind her ear.

"Is this the royal 'we'? " Gabrielle started to ask, but Mason moved his hand to cup her chin. She leaned into the kiss, resting her hands on his shoulders as the kiss deepened. Her pulse quickened.

Mason pulled back. "An absolute villain," he said, breathless. "We should finish the movie so I can get you home." Mason leaned back against the couch but made a space for Gabrielle to tuck in under his arm. She tried not to show her disappointment as she curled up against him.

Gabrielle woke up to a flurry of activity as Mason rushed around his hotel room wearing only an open bathrobe and boxer briefs, his hair still wet from a shower. "Did we fall asleep?" she asked, yawning. "What time is it?"

"My flight leaves in under an hour," Mason said as he shrugged off his bathrobe, giving Gabrielle just enough time to admire his lean but muscular torso before he slipped into a clean shirt. "I hate to do this, but I can call for a cab to take you back to your apartment."

"Maybe Sean can pick me up," Gabrielle said. She stood and walked across the room, pulling her phone from Sean's jacket. A few calls, a voice message, and several increasingly colorful texts confirmed Sean was worried. Shoot. She should have known.

"The room's paid for through next week." Mason stopped getting ready long enough to kiss Gabrielle on the cheek as she sat back down. "Take all the time you need."

"Where the hell are you?" Sean asked after Gabrielle dialed.

"Mason's hotel," she answered, cringing.

"You minx!" Sean's initial anger gave way to enthusiasm. "Tell me everything when you get back."

"Yeah, about that," Gabrielle said. "Mason has to leave for a surprise interview in New York City, and he's sort of running late, so I was wondering if you could come get me."

"Ugh, fine." Gabrielle could almost hear Sean roll his eyes over the phone. "But then I want details."

"I can't wait to see you when I get back." Mason gave Gabrielle another kiss, this time on the lips, before shouldering a duffle bag on his way out the door. She felt a pang of longing as the door closed behind him and, beneath that, a growing sense of trepidation for reasons she couldn't identify.

eighteen

"I'M sorry I interrupted your nap, but I really did need help with the grocery shopping," Sean said a few hours later. He slid a case of bottled water onto the bottom of the cart while Gabrielle pushed.

"It's fine," Gabrielle said around a yawn. "A dose of normalcy will probably do me good after last night." She pushed the cart into a lane, but Sean stopped her.

"We should go in that lane instead." He pointed a row over.

"Why? This one is shorter." Gabrielle raised an eyebrow.

"Yeah, but how many times have we made that mistake before?" Sean scratched the back of his head as he floundered for a rationale. "It's like every time we go to Canada. We always pick the lane that looks shortest, and it backfires every time."

"Sometimes it works out," Gabrielle said, thinking of her evening with Mason. "Besides, this is a grocery store, not Customs."

The shopper in front of Gabrielle moved forward. He began to empty the contents of his cart onto the conveyor belt. A row over, the cashier called for a price check. Gabrielle gave Sean her"I told you so" look. He stood awkwardly with his back to the magazine rack.

Weird.

Sean could be described as many things, but seldom was he awkward.

"Sean, why are you blocking the magazines?"

Gabrielle heard snickering a few aisles away. She noticed a couple teenage girls looking in their direction. She turned back to Sean, folding her arms across her chest. With a heavy sigh of defeat, he moved out of her way. Gabrielle's eyes widened. She pushed past him to pick up a gossip rag with her picture – *her* picture, not the doppelgänger's – in the bottom corner.

The caption read "This Week's Walk of Shame," promising more details on page 5. She flipped to that page. Sean read over her shoulder:

Bri Johnson, a wannabe starlet who scored a small part in a new movie being shot in Western New York, was seen leaving up-and-coming Holly-wood heartthrob Mason Wright's hotel late last night. The bad news for everyone crushing on Mason is things appear to be heating up. The good news is, this makeup-free picture means us normal girls have a shot when the whirlwind romance comes to an inevitable end.

"It could have been worse." Sean placed a reassuring hand on Gabrielle's shoulder.

"Worse than the other me finding out I was with him?" Gabrielle hissed under her breath. "There's no way she's not going to find out about this, Sean. And that's bad for him and me, both." She handed him the magazine and began to move groceries onto the conveyor belt.

"Uh oh."

Gabrielle looked back at Sean. She knew they were thinking the same thing. The doppelgänger was not the only person she needed to worry about. They jumped when her phone rang. Gabrielle slipped it out of her back pocket, hands shaking.

"Your mother?"

"My mother."

. . .

An hour later, Gabrielle sank onto the futon. She pulled a throw pillow under her head and rubbed her face with one of her hands. "Sorry I wasn't more help unloading the groceries," she said.

"No biggie. Did you manage to talk her down?"

"I think she just ran out of steam," Gabrielle said. "She wouldn't even believe me when I told her nothing happened, nothing more than kissing anyway, just like she didn't believe me about Brandon."

"But something did happen with Brandon," Sean said. "Just not with *you* you."

"And if I tried to tell her about that, she would have me institutionalized. Instead, she's just trying to make me come home." Gabrielle sighed. "And then I'd have to have myself institutionalized."

"So, this might be a wacky notion, but have you considered reminding your mother that you're a grown ass adult who can make her own decisions?"

Gabrielle was about to answer when her phone rang. She rolled her eyes at Sean, pushing herself up into a seated position. She had no desire to go any more rounds with her mother, but she pulled the phone out of her back pocket. It was her father calling instead.

"Hello?"

"Hey, hon. It's me. Your dad."

Gabrielle laughed. "I know your voice, Dad. Besides, it shows me your number when you call. It's programmed into my phone." She paused. "Did Mom make you call?"

"No, no. I'm calling of my own free will. Your mom is doing some work in her office now. I just...I just wanted to see if you were okay. Been seeing wild stories on the news, and after spring break...I don't know. You just seemed...different, somehow."

Gabrielle smiled, blinking back unexpected tears. "I'm fine, Dad. It's been kind of a weird few weeks for me."

"Yeah, your mom and I never knew you had the acting bug. I still remember the time you were the Christmas tree in the school play and fainted dead away when the curtain rose."

A few tears spilled down Gabrielle's cheeks as she laughed. "I think little Jacob Sawyer shouting 'Timber!' was a nice touch, though. The audience never had to know it wasn't in the script."

Mr. Johnson chuckled. "So, this Mason character. Is he...is he nice to you?"

"He's very nice to me." Gabrielle smiled. "Try not to worry too much about whatever the news is saying. You know how they like to hype things up for money. He has been nothing but a perfect gentleman, no matter how it looks on TV or in the magazines."

"Okay, after the whole thing with Brandon, I just wanted to be sure things were okay."

"Dad, I promise you nothing happened with Brandon."

"You've got a good head on your shoulders. I wanted you to know that. I'm proud of you, kiddo."

"Thanks, Dad."

"Your mother is proud of you, too," Mr. Johnson added. "She'd never admit it to you, but she's been bragging to everyone at work about the movie. I think she worries because you go where angels fear to tread. Take care of yourself, okay?"

"Always."

Sean went out with Lance, so Gabrielle had the apartment to herself. She tried to work on her research paper, but she was too worried to concentrate. She had not heard from Mason all day. She considered sending a text to warn him about the tabloid, but she figured his publicist and agent would be all over it.

Maybe Mason was angry she let herself be photographed—though Gabrielle had not noticed anyone when she waited outside the hotel for Sean. He couldn't blame her for it. But maybe he had decided that trying to date her would be more trouble than she was worth. Filming was finished next week anyway.

Even watching Tiffany Sharp's music videos, one of which was like a mini-action movie that fit right into her research paper's premise, failed to distract Gabrielle from her worries. When the doorbell rang, she felt the tiniest twinge of hope. Maybe it was Mason. A relieved smile spread across her face when she left her room to open the door.

She should have looked out the peephole first.

It wasn't Mason.

It was *her*.

nineteen

THE DOPPELGÄNGER STROLLED into the living room, dressed simply in a navy shift that Gabrielle remembered from her shopping excursion with her mother, with black flats and a designer handbag. Despite the chilly evening air, the doppelgänger's bare arms appeared smooth. A predatory grin spread across the woman's face as she sat down on the armchair. Not knowing what else to do, Gabrielle walked behind the futon, tightly gripping the back. From this close, she could see all the little adjustments her doppelgänger had made. No smattering of freckles over her nose and cheeks. Darker blue eyes. Longer lashes. Larger breasts. And that same absence of pores that had given Lance away.

They were otherwise identical. It gave Gabrielle the creeps.

"So...how long have you been back?" her doppelgänger asked with a drawn-out conversational brightness to her voice, as though Gabrielle had returned from an extended vacation and not an endless slumber in whatever hellish world she had been left in.

"About a week ago," Gabrielle said. "I woke up in the middle of the woods. A couple of hunters found me. I called Sean. He brought me home." She left out the part about Lance being the one who rescued her. She did not know what, if anything, her doppelgänger knew about him or about the federal agents who weren't really federal agents.

"Huh," her doppelgänger said, considering her story. "And what have you been doing all this time? I know I haven't seen you at work." Her grin widened.

"Trying to figure out what you've been doing," Gabrielle said. "I know *you* haven't been going to school. They were about to kick me out of all my classes." Though she still felt uneasy, Gabrielle loosened her grip on the futon. She stepped from behind the futon and sat down.

"Yes, well, I was moving onto bigger and better things. Who needs a degree when you're destined for stardom?" The doppelgänger leaned back in her armchair. "You know, it wouldn't be the worst arrangement if the two of us continued living as one person, and you and your roommate kept your mouths shut about it. You could do all the boring academic stuff. I could focus on our budding career in film."

Gabrielle raised an eyebrow, doubtful.

"There's just one problem with that idea." The doppelgänger's tone darkened.

"And what's that?" Gabrielle asked. She tried not to show her discomfort. She did not know the extent of the doppelgänger's supernatural abilities. Avoiding any tasty offerings might not be enough to stay out of harm's way.

"I don't like to share," the doppelgänger said. Her predatory grin faded as she narrowed her eyes, but she looked no less dangerous.

"That is a problem," Gabrielle agreed.

The smile returned to the doppelgänger's face. "Fortunately, I think I might have a solution that benefits both of us. You see, I'm not from around here, as you've probably figured out, and I've got these...friends from back home. I think your roommate met them already. Anyway, they're anxious for me to return, but I have my own plans."

"Which are?"

"That's where things have gotten tricky," the doppelgänger said. "I was going to use you to break into the business, but they're onto me, and I'm running out of time. Now that I have access to people a little higher on the food chain, I can transform into someone else and restore your life to you in full. You can have it all: your newfound celebrity to do with as you will, the paycheck, even Mason. I'm sure a rising star like Natalia could snag even better eye candy."

Gabrielle gasped when she realized the implication of the doppelgänger's words. "How would that protect you from your 'friends' from home?"

"You see, they like to keep our existence in your world a secret. And since I'm unauthorized, I needed to keep my existence a secret from *them*. My exit from life as Simone was too sloppy. I should have waited until she faded into obscurity, but I could not stand another moment living life as an older woman." The doppelgänger stood. She walked behind the futon, placing her hands on Gabrielle's shoulder.

Gabrielle tried not to flinch as she noticed how dangerously long and pointed the doppelgänger's cherry red nails were as they sank into her shoulders. Gabrielle braced herself, but the other woman only gave them a gentle squeeze.

"You're too young to understand," her doppelgänger continued, "but humans – *men* – stop paying attention to women once you reach a certain age. All I had left before me were years of meeting housewives and divorcés desperate to turn their lives around...or pushy career women hoping to fix their directionless daughters at book signings until even they lose interest and move on to the next big thing." The doppelgänger let go of Gabrielle's shoulders and came around to sit beside her on the futon. "But it's all going to work out because you're back, and now I can disappear into someone else's life."

"What makes you think I'll play along?"

"I'm a powerful friend to have on your side," the doppelgänger said, caressing Gabrielle's cheek. "You once told me that you wanted to be a director. Don't you think an actress of Natalia's stature could make that happen? And think of Mason. I know you like him. Who wouldn't? What a fine power couple the two of you would make." She paused, raising an eyebrow. "What did you tell him, anyway? He can't possibly think we're the same person."

"That you're my long-lost identical twin sister trying to take over my life," Gabrielle said.

"The 'evil twin' trope? Really?" Her doppelgänger shuddered with distaste. "Oh well. It'll be up to you to sort that one out." She patted Gabrielle's knee, then stood and went to the door.

Gabrielle rose to follow her.

"Oh, there's one more thing." The doppelgänger turned to face her. "I'll need your help getting Natalia alone. Apparently the two of you really hit it off at that party last night, and she invited us to go shopping tomorrow afternoon!" she said with mock cheerfulness. "I don't know if I can pull off that sweet demure routine you've got going on as well as you can, so I need you to go in my stead and get her to come back to my apartment."

"And if I don't agree?"

"I can be a powerful enemy, too, Bri," the doppelgänger said, reaching out to tuck a strand of Gabrielle's hair behind her ear, "but I think you already know that. You have tonight to think about it. I'll talk to you first thing in the morning. If you have any questions, you know where to reach me." She reached into her handbag and pulled out an envelope, handing it to Gabrielle. "As a gesture of good will, I'm leaving you this gift. You'll need it tomorrow."

Gabrielle watched as the doppelgänger opened the door and left. She looked down at the envelope in her hand. It bulged in the center and jangled when she shook it. Sure enough, she opened the envelope to find the keys to her car and the apartment. *She could have waited until I slept to come in and finish the job she left to those awful creatures*, Gabrielle realized. Except her doppelgänger's plan hinged on leaving Gabrielle alive...for now. That plan might change if she did not play along.

And she wouldn't.
She couldn't.

twenty

GABRIELLE WAS STILL LYING awake in her bed when she heard Sean come in from his date with Lance. She considered telling him about her encounter with the doppelgänger but decided against it. She could fill him in tomorrow morning. No sense in spoiling his evening.

Lance was the one she really wanted to talk to about her dilemma. He knew about the doppelgänger. He'd rescued her from that other world. He must be one of the "friends" the doppelgänger spoke of, along with the federal agents who weren't really federal agents.

Agent Buzz Cut and Agent Mustache — is that what Sean had called them?

The three had to be planning something, but what?

And would they do it before it was too late?

At some point Gabrielle slipped into a restless sleep. Along with the now-usual images of alien landscapes, she saw the accusing faces of Mason and Natalia, the latter as she was pulled into a writhing swarm of monsters with sharp fangs and glowing eyes. Even Tiffany

Sharp made a cameo, outfitted in a dark wig, sleek leather catsuit, and knee-high stiletto boots, as she took a flamethrower to the swarm.

Of all the stupidest dreams, Gabrielle thought upon awakening. Then she groaned as she remembered the real events of the night before and her doppelgänger's ultimatum. No way would she allow that part of the dream to come true.

She sat up and reached for her phone on the nightstand, then dialed her old number. Her doppelgänger answered on the second ring. "Natalia wants us to meet her at the hotel by noon. Humor her for a bit, then invite her to our place for a drink. I'll send you a text with the address. You should map it first so you don't make her suspicious."

"You'll have to tell her that you aren't feeling well, and that you have to cancel," Gabrielle said. "I'm not going."

The doppelgänger was silent.

"Hello? Are you still there? I'm. Not. Going."

"I heard you the first time," the doppelgänger snapped. "Okay, then. Change of plans." Gabrielle could hear the smile in her voice as she purred, "I'll send Mason your regards."

Gabrielle stared at the phone.

What did *that* mean?

Gabrielle scrolled through her recent calls until she found the number Mason had used to call her Friday. She fired off a text:

Mason? It's Bri. My sister knows. She's really angry. I don't know what she's going to do. No matter what she says or does, avoid her. Even if she says she's me. Just...stay away.

Gabrielle could feel any chances of a relationship slipping away as she sent the text, but Mason's safety was more important. Whatever the doppelgänger's new plan was, it couldn't be good. For any of them. She stared at the phone, her heart racing. Moments later she saw the telltale dots that showed Mason was in the process of responding.

Relax. I have a photoshoot 4 the magazine 2day. I fly back later 2night. If it makes you feel better, I'll come straight 2 your apartment. I get in around 10.

More dots.

She's just a girl. We'll figure this out. 2gether.

Gabrielle smiled despite herself. Then she tried to contact Natalia, but the hotel was unwilling to put a call through.

* * *

"Hey, you," Sean said when Gabrielle emerged from the bathroom in a sweatshirt and rumply shorts, her hair wet from showering. "I have to go to work today. There's a lot of dresses and suits that need to be steamed and sorted before they shoot the prom scenes this week."

"She came to see me last night," Gabrielle said, slumping into the chair across from him as he reclined on the futon, typing something on his phone.

Sean looked up. "Who...? Oh. Oh!" He sat up, setting his phone down. "How did *that* go?"

"She wanted me to help her become Natalia instead. You know those fake agents you told me about? She calls them her friends from back home, wherever *that* is. I guess she thinks switching to Natalia will get them off her back without attracting any more attention. She even gave me back my car as a gesture of goodwill or whatever." Gabrielle half-smiled, but it did not reach her eyes.

"You didn't agree to do it, did you?" Sean's eyes widened.

Gabrielle glared. "Of course not."

"Do you think she'll try to go after Natalia anyway?"

"I don't know," Gabrielle said with a tremor in her voice. "She threatened Mason. I think she's going to try to do something to him to force my hand. Or maybe she can go after Natalia with or without my help. It's all so crazy. I don't know what to do." She ran her hands through her wet hair.

"I know you can't say anything to Natalia, but did you warn Mason?" Sean rose from the futon. He walked behind Gabrielle's chair and rested his hands on her shoulders.

Gabrielle lifted her head. "Yeah, he's coming straight here from the airport. Around 10, I think."

"Sit tight until then. If those fake agents are still roaming around, I don't think she can do anything too risky." Sean gave her shoulders a reassuring squeeze.

After Sean left, the hours crept by. Gabrielle tried to work on her research paper some more. She made it to the seventh page before she ran out of steam. Her meeting wasn't for another three days. Surely, that was enough time to write the last three pages of her rough draft, save an actress from a doppelgänger, and get the guy...

...right?

Gabrielle groaned. She laid her head down on the desk beside her laptop.

"I thought you were good people," Natalia said in an accusing tone. *Blood stained the translucent sleeves of her white jumpsuit. Her brown skin had grown ashen and sallow, her cheeks sunken. Glittering dark eyes glared at Gabrielle from behind lifeless brown tangles.*

"You'll never be the leading lady."

Tiffany appeared behind Natalia, once again outfitted in black leather. She picked at her nails with a long, jagged dagger. "You don't have the strength." She tossed the dagger at Gabrielle's head.

Gabrielle ducked.

The doppelgänger chuckled. "You'll never be anyone.*"*

Gabrielle turned to face her. A monster with sharp fangs and glowing eyes sat on her shoulder. The doppelgänger stroked its mottled flesh lovingly. Another monster crawled from behind the doppelgänger's leg, rubbing its misshapen head against her calf as it mewled. The monster on the doppelgänger's shoulder opened its jaws wide and screeched before launching itself at Gabrielle. Still more monsters poured out of the shadows. Gabrielle clutched at her head as she fell to her knees.

"No, no..."

"No!"

Gabrielle had fallen asleep at her desk with her head buried in her arms. She rubbed at her face, a kink stretching in her neck, then ran her fingers through her disheveled curls before pushing back the lid of her laptop to check the time.

Only seven.

She sighed. Her phone beeped.

Gabrielle clicked on a text from Sean:

Natalia came for a last-minute fitting. She seems...fine. I think.

Gabrielle sighed with relief. Natalia was okay. For now, anyway. The sooner she figured out what to do about her doppelgänger, the safer they all would be. She still wanted to talk to Lance, but the Loft was closed on Sunday and Monday, and she had no idea how to contact him without asking Sean.

Gabrielle hated keeping Lance's real identity a secret from her best friend, not that she knew who – or what – he really was. She would have to pressure Lance to tell Sean himself. A half-hour of searching online brought her no closer to reaching out to Lance. He did not have a social media presence that she could find, unless he kept it hidden, even from Sean. Her own social media accounts had not been updated by the doppelgänger in days. She closed her laptop.

The clock read half past eleven when the doorbell finally rang. Her phone beeped a moment later.

It's me.

Gabrielle rose from the futon, where she had dozed since giving up her search for Lance. She peered through the peephole before opening the door. Mason began to kiss her as soon as he entered the apartment. She reached back to close the door with one hand before wrapping her arms around his back.

"I was so worried," Gabrielle said in between kisses as they sank onto the futon. She gasped when Mason bit her lip, hard enough to draw blood. Only then did she pull away. She scrambled off the futon and took a step back.

"Where is he?"

twenty-one

THE DOPPELGÄNGER GRINNED up at Gabrielle with Mason's face as it lounged on the futon, its eyes as cold and dispassionate as a shark's. "I think you already know."

"What do you want?" Gabrielle sat across from not-Mason on the armchair, willing her legs to stop shaking as she pressed her hands against her knees.

"Only your continued cooperation," not-Mason said with a sly smile, draping his arms over the back of the futon. He gave Gabrielle a look of sympathy, adding, "I'm sorry you blew your chance at winning the guy. It's not like the *whirlwind romance* was going to last, though, was it? Sooner or later, he'd grow tired of you and meet someone else on the road. Or maybe you'd just push him away worrying about it. The anxiety of dating a Hollywood heartthrob would do more to distract you from your career than further it. And Mother's so very anxious for you to make something of yourself, isn't she?"

Gabrielle glared. The truth was, she hadn't thought any further than protecting Mason from her doppelgänger. Now it was too late, and she did not know where to go from there. She just knew that she wanted Mason to be safe, with or without her.

"I can still help," not-Mason continued in a shallow approxima-tion of the real Mason's accent. "We would, of course, tell anyone who asks that we're still really good friends even if it didn't work out, and I'd put in a good word for you with Hollywood's heaviest hitters. You don't have to come out of this a loser. Work with me, we both win."

"What about Mason?"

Not-Mason sighed in exasperation. "What about him? I'm offering you the world. Don't screw this up, Bri. Not again."

"If you're so powerful and influential, why stop at Hollywood? Why not set your sights on something bigger, like *real* world leader-ship?" Gabrielle narrowed her eyes. "Or is that your next step?"

Not-Mason frowned. "There are some lines even I won't cross. I just want to enjoy your world," he drawled, the smile returning to his face. "I don't need to rule it."

Gabrielle did not know what to say to that.

Non-Mason rose from the couch to leave. "Don't try to find Mason," he said. "Besides, my world's not all bad. Maybe I left him somewhere nice." He reached into his back pocket to remove a couple of folded pages. "You may want to learn your lines before Thursday. You won't be doing your career any favors if you screw up your last day of filming. You won't even need to dig deep for your performance. You just have to admit defeat."

Not-Mason gave Gabrielle another mocking look of feigned sympathy. Then he leaned down to kiss the top of her head as he dropped the papers onto her lap.

Gabrielle was still sitting in the chair when Sean came home, her eyes vacant as she stared across the room at nothing in particular.

"Prom scenes are the worst," Sean said as he removed the jacket he wore over a dark brown sweater. "Some of the looks the extras brought. My God." He hung his jacket on the hook by the door. "Like, don't get me wrong, those two extras may have had the bodies for something really slinky or sheer with strategically placed rhine-stones, but we're aiming for PG-13 here, and there's limits to what I can do with fabric tape."

Still oblivious to Gabrielle's silence, Sean slipped off his shoes and fell back onto the futon. "And nobody can pull off hot pink sequined taffe..." Sean stopped in the middle of his rant when he noticed Gabrielle. "What's wrong?"

Gabrielle turned her head to meet Sean's look of concern, her eyes still glazed from shock. "He's gone."

Sean sat up. "Well, I'm sure you'll see him again later this week," he said. Gabrielle only continued to stare through him. Recognizing the depths of her despair, he asked, "Did he decide that he's mad about your pretend sister after all?"

"No. Mason is gone like I was gone." Gabrielle squeezed her eyes shut for a few moments before opening them as she ran her hands through her hair. She no longer appeared lost, but the sense of despair remained. "The doppelgänger made the transformation, but into Mason instead of Natalia. I don't know how it happened. She must have caught up with him at the airport and convinced him she was me." Gabrielle looked at Sean. "We have to talk to Lance. Now. There isn't any time."

Sean furrowed his eyebrows, unnerved. "What does Lance have to do with anything?"

Gabrielle took a deep breath. "Lance's the one who found me," she said as she sat beside Sean. "He...he's not from around here, either. I'm sorry. I should have said something sooner." She reached for Sean's hand, but he pulled it away.

"How long have you known?" Sean rose from the futon, shoving his hands into the pockets of his jeans.

"I had my suspicions when you showed me his picture," Gabrielle said, "but I knew for sure when you brought me to meet him. He made me promise not to say anything, and I didn't know how to tell you, but I should have said something that very night. I know that now."

"So, he's like her," Sean said. He looked at Gabrielle, his green eyes darkening. "Who do you think he was?" he asked softly. "The real Lance, I mean. The one whose life he stole."

"He didn't steal anyone's life," Gabrielle said. "Lance told me that he was...authorized...to be here. The other one wasn't. That's why she needs to steal existing identities. But I don't know who authorizes it, or why they come here, or even what they are."

"So, what makes you think he was telling you the truth?" Sean paced across the carpet. . "He lied about who he was. How do you know he wasn't lying about that, too?"

"I saw him," Gabrielle said, her eyes glazing over as she lost herself in the memory. "It was only for a moment, and then I think I screamed and fainted, but I saw him, Sean. The bone structure, the body, it was the same. Only his skin looked different." She shivered. "It was so translucent, he looked almost blue, like you could see every vein and artery. Their world—I don't think it gets a lot of sunlight."

Sean stopped his pacing to collapse into the armchair. "So, they're still humanoid, whatever they are." He looked up at Gabrielle. "It's not entirely some sort of illusion."

"He is," Gabrielle said. "Whatever fed on me in his world wasn't."

Sean lifted his head sharply.

"There were these creatures, feeding on me, draining my blood. They kept me warm and alive, I think, but also unconscious and trapped in this weird dream state." Gabrielle shuddered. "I'm afraid that's where Mason is now."

Sean stood again, reaching his hand out to Gabrielle. "Then we're going to see Lance. Tonight. You deserve answers." His eyes narrowed. "We both do."

* * *

Lance lived in a quiet neighborhood just outside of Buffalo. His home was two stories but narrow, with a small front yard, one-car driveway, and neighboring homes within a few feet on either side. Though the neighborhood was not affluent, the yards were well kept. Even Lance maintained a pretty little garden of irises in front of a modest covered porch. A windchime with dangling pieces of multi-colored glass tinkled in the breeze.

Sean knocked on the door.

Lance did not look as surprised to see them as Gabrielle expected. Instead, his strange amber eyes appeared resigned and more than a little sad as he ushered them into the home.

The modest exterior did not prepare Gabrielle for the grandeur inside. Though Lance's home was small, everything about its interior conveyed opulence, perhaps even wealth. The walls were painted an unusual color that wasn't quite blue, green, or gray, with a glossy sheen. Paintings of other worlds in ornate frames accented the walls. The hardwood floor glistened. A plush couch of emerald-green suede sat on a plush cream rug highlighted with specs of crimson, gold, green, and blue opposite a wall with a recessed fireplace. The side table and coffee table appeared to be ivory marble with veins of gold and silver.

Next to the side table was an oversized chair of the same emerald-green suede. That was where Lance sat as he gestured to the couch. Gabrielle sat, though Sean remained standing near the front door, his arms folded across his chest and his green eyes revealing nothing of the turmoil behind them.

Gabrielle's eyes wandered to the partial partition that separated the living room from the kitchen. She could see the glimmering marble countertops and a backsplash of gold, silver, and crystalline stones. Lance came from such a shadowy world, she supposed it only made sense for him to fill his new world with so much color and light. Still, her eyes were drawn to one painting of a dark landscape filled with phosphorescent trees and strange glowing ponds. The night sky was filled with stars, but also bands of green and magenta light.

That's his home.

Were the other paintings of real places, too?

Gabrielle was about to lose herself in another painting, this one depicting an impossibly blue ocean of unfamiliar sea creatures, some as big as whales, benevolent yet unafraid. Humanoid beings swam among them, all strange and glowing.

Lance interrupted her silence to say, "She's assumed her next identity, then?"

Gabrielle nodded.

"Natalia Martinez?"

"No, Mason."

Now Lance appeared surprised. "I hadn't anticipated that move. I don't know why she thinks assuming the identity of a celebrity will shield her from us when filming is almost over, anyway. We can restore Mason to his life without most of the complications we would have had with you. Unless..."

"Unless she doesn't expect you to find Mason as easily as you found me," Gabrielle finished for him.

"Or there's no Mason left to find," Sean added, his tone dark. He sat beside Gabrielle on the couch, putting a hand on her shoulder. "Sorry, Bri." He turned to Lance. "I just think it's time for everyone to be completely honest about everything that's happening and what's really at stake here."

"I kept secrets from you, and I'm sorry," Lance said to Sean. "As long as I've been living among humans, I sometimes forget I'm not one of you."

"My ex kept secrets," Sean said. "This is a bit bigger than that, don't you think?"

"Yes," Lance agreed. "And there's still so little I can tell you, which is all the more reason I should never have let things get this far." He gazed across the room of a painting depicting a girl reaching to her reflection in a pond. "There are...*others* of my kind who build their lives with humans, but most long-term relationships are discouraged, if not forbidden."

"That sounds rather dramatic," Gabrielle said. She realized the hand reaching back in the painting was not the girl's reflection, but another being entirely. She shivered.

"Not nearly as dramatic as what can happen when rules are broken. The rules exist for a reason," Lance said. "All I can tell you, and I shouldn't even be telling you this, is that I come from a dying world. Beings from my world discovered vortices to your world when they were driven below ground by what you would call the red giant stage of our sun. Now that our sun is a white dwarf, our world is cooling beyond our capacity to evolve, even with all of our...special talents."

"Meanwhile, ours is heating up," Sean said.

"Which is concerning," Lance agreed.

Gabrielle remembered her conversation with not-Mason. "Can't you use your special talents and your influence to, like, I dunno, save us from ourselves?" she asked.

"Sounds great in theory, but the last time someone from my world sought to influence someone in yours, it went...poorly. She was betrayed, rewritten in history as the villain, and ultimately written out of history as a myth," Lance said. "She began developing a system for helping beings from my world move into yours, as long as we play nice and don't draw too much attention to ourselves. Once upon a time she tried to help a king imagine a better world. Now she's saving us from ours through human-inspired bureaucracy." His smile was bitter.

"Ironic," Gabrielle said, her head spinning. "So...is she, like, in charge in your world? She must be hundreds of years old." *At least.* Gabrielle cast a sidelong glance at Sean. How old was Lance?

"She rules our world alongside two sisters," Lance said.

"I'm not sure if I should be more horrified by nepotism or by the super-centralized government," Gabrielle said, grinning as she tried to wrap her brain around the thought of another world governed in its entirety by three seemingly immortal sisters.

"Hey, you only have, like, half a dozen CEOs running your

world," Lance said, returning her smile. "And they are way less conscientious of their global impact. Don't judge."

Sean had been quiet through their exchange, but now he looked at Lance, his green eyes blazing with anger. "And you're one of the bureaucrats, aren't you?"

Lance's smile faded.

"Let me guess," Sean continued. "You're in charge of investigating unauthorized otherworldly immigrants before they give up the game. Were you just using me to find the doppelgänger?"

Lance sighed. "No," he said. "No, that was a weirdly helpful coincidence. We knew we were close to catching her, but we didn't know who her latest victim was until you started telling me about Gabrielle, and I did the math. My interest in you was...*is*...genuine."

Gabrielle felt Sean stiffen beside her. She reached for his hand, squeezing it. After a moment, Sean squeezed back. She gave him a sympathetic smile before turning back to Lance.

"How did you find me?"

"We found the remains of her last two victims in our world near vortices where they had last been seen in yours. She always left them in wild places where others would dispose of them instead of doing the dirty work herself. Subterranean pools, scorched forests that have been reinhabited by the more vile creatures in our world." Lance's brow furrowed. "You're the first victim I found alive."

Gabrielle frowned. "I don't want to be the last."

"You won't," Lance's tone was resolute. "She didn't have time to travel too far out of this region, so there are only a few places to look. I can check the more...*time-sensitive* places tonight. You two should go home, get some rest. Let me take care of it from here."

"I want to go with you," Gabrielle said.

Lance shook his head. "It's too dangerous. You're not even supposed to know my world exists, let alone go there. Besides, if I'm too late...you don't want to see the things I've seen, Bri. I mean it. It's hard enough for me. I don't share the emotional connection you have with Mason."

"I can't just do nothing," Gabrielle said.

Sean put his arm around her shoulder. "He's right, Bri."

Gabrielle ignored him.

"Please?" she said to Lance, her eyes pleading.

Lance sighed. "I'll tell you what. If I haven't found him elsewhere, I'll let you come with me to the place I found you. The danger isn't as great. If that's where she left him, time is on our side...and his."

Sean helped a reluctant Gabrielle to her feet. They walked to the door. Lance stood. "Sean, I-"

"Just find Mason," Sean said without looking back. "That's all that matters right now."

Sean was silent as he started the car. After driving for a few minutes, he turned to Gabrielle and said, "The Lady in the Lake."

Gabrielle looked over at him, confused. "We're not even by the lake. What lady?"

"No, that story Lance told us. I think he was talking about the Lady in the Lake." Sean narrowed his eyes as he thought. "She was, like, a witch, or a fairy, or something, and she gave King Arthur his sword, Excalibur. Then she turned Merlin into a tree for breaking up with her. I think. This girl I dated in high school was obsessed with those stories. She always said that the lady got a raw deal, too. I helped her make a dress for a festival once."

Gabrielle furrowed her brow as she tried to make sense of his words. "Sean, are you trying to tell me that Lance...and the actor formerly known as my doppelgänger...that they're, like...fairies?" She raised an eyebrow.

Sean looked at her. "I think so..." he said, shaking his head as though he could not believe it himself.

"I figured they were aliens," Gabrielle said.

Sean shrugged. "I'm not sure the distinction matters."

"How...how serious were things getting?" Gabrielle asked, her voice softening. "Between you and Lance?"

"I don't want to talk about it," Sean said. "Not right now. It's a lot to process. But I'm not mad at you for not telling me. Not anymore. I'm not sure I would have believed you if you had, even knowing what I already knew. Except..."

"Except what?" Gabrielle gently prodded.

"On some level, I think I knew he was...*different*," Sean said. "I just didn't want to believe it, and not because of what it meant for me and him. Our world just got a whole lot bigger, Bri, and it's not just *our* world anymore, you know?"

"Worlds," Gabrielle said. "It's worlds. And they didn't come to ours by a spaceship, but a...what? A vortex? Is that like a wormhole or something? Are Lance and those fake agents and the doppelgänger even from the same universe?"

Sean grimaced. "Like I said, it's a lot."

This time when Gabrielle dreamt of that familiar alien landscape, she happened upon a luminescent pond. Her reflection grinned up at her. And it really was her, right down to the smattering of freckles across her nose. She extended a hand. The water was warm, like a hot spring. It rippled around her fingertips, distorting her reflection.

The face that grinned up at Gabrielle was no longer her own. The graying lips parted to reveal jagged blood-stained teeth as a strong claw-like hand grasped at her wrist. She screamed as it pulled her into the pond. The once shallow body of water expanded into a deep sea filled with unearthly creatures, some as big as whales, none benevolent. She choked on water as she swam up to the surface.

Mason stared down at her. She reached out for him, but he pushed down on top of her head instead, holding her under. Something large and rough, with scales like sandpaper, brushed against her legs as she struggled. The world went dark.

twenty-two

"YOU LOOK LIKE HELL," Monica said as she sat next to Gabrielle in class the following morning.

"Thanks," Gabrielle said. "You're a special friend." She sat with her chin resting on the palm of her hand as she struggled to stay awake during her discussion group.

Gabrielle slipped through the rest of the day in a daze. Her legs had been tangled in the sheets when she woke up that morning, and she hit her head when she fell out of bed. If anyone noticed the goose egg she'd tried in vain to cover with her hair, they demonstrated more tact than Monica possessed and kept it to themselves.

"Anything yet?" Sean looked as tired as Gabrielle felt when he caught up with her in the parking garage. Even though she had her car back, they'd still ridden to campus together.

"Not yet," Gabrielle said. "This is why I wanted to go with him. I hate not knowing."

Her phone beeped in the pocket of her hoodie. She exchanged a look with Sean as she pulled it out. "It's Lance."

No luck yet. Meet me at my place.

Dress warm.

"Did you expect anything different?" Sean asked.

"No," Gabrielle said, turning to him. "It's always going to be in the last place you look."

The day was unseasonably warm, which was unfortunate. Gabrielle left the apartment with thermal underwear beneath her jeans and hoodie, a long winter coat draped over her arm. By the time she arrived at Lance's home, an annoying trickle of sweat was dripping down her back.

"We'll take my car," Lance said as he met her outside. Gabrielle looked at him in his tee shirt and jeans, envious.

"Hope we don't run into too many people out for a hike," she said as she slid into the passenger seat of his car, a Honda Civic like hers, but much newer. To her amusement, a Tiffany Sharp song came on the radio, an overwrought ballad instead of her usual upbeat dance songs. "Is she one of yours?" Gabrielle asked.

Lance laughed as he started the car. "Despite her infamous otherworldly persona, Tiffany Sparks is one hundred percent human. Maybe even one hundred and ten percent."

"She's a little extra," Gabrielle agreed.

"Do you know her?" Lance asked.

"I actually do, believe it or not." A funny thing to say under the circumstances, Gabrielle realized. "Mason took me to a party she threw the other night." It had only been a couple days since the party, but it felt like an eternity. So much had changed in such a short amount of time. "Meeting her should have been the craziest thing that's ever happened to me, and yet..."

Lance gave her a sympathetic smile.

They drove in companionable silence for a long while before Lance asked, "How is he?"

"Reeling," Gabrielle said. "We both are. It was...," she paused, gazing out the window. They had left the city and suburbs behind.

Now Lance drove past farms, fields, and the occasional rural town. "It's a lot," she finished.

Lance slowed the car as he drove past a small herd of deer grazing in an open meadow between the road and tree line. Gabrielle noticed him wince when he saw a dead raccoon along the side of the road.

"Our world's a lot different from yours, isn't it?" Gabrielle asked. Now she was the one to wince. *What a stupid question.*

"We developed magic like you have technology," Lance said seriously, as if he did not agree with her internal assessment. "I imagine somewhere exists a world with a mix of both. Maybe even capabilities neither of our worlds have words to describe. Any number of possibilities, really."

Gabrielle shivered at the implication. "How does your magic still work in our world?"

"It's not as strong here," Lance said. "There are limits to what we can do on Earth. I don't know the physics behind it." He chuckled. "That's above my pay grade. But I suspect it's taking even more of her energy to maintain the illusion of being Mason instead of another woman. Natalia would have been a little closer to her in height, too."

"So it's an illusion?" Gabrielle asked. "She's not, like, a shapeshifter or something? How come it still works on camera?"

"A little of both," Lance said. "We can easily maintain a complete transformation on our own world." He turned to Gabrielle. "I'm sorry I didn't have my human appearance when I found you. I didn't expect you to wake up so soon." His eyes returned to the road. "Anyway, here our magic is less stable. It can get distorted, like a bad radio transmission. Even more so when the illusion is so different from our natural state."

Gabrielle remembered her visit with Simone and that occasional shimmering blue tone her skin had taken. In retrospect, it reminded her of when she would try to adjust the antennae - or what her parents called "rabbit ears" - on an old television set her grandparents had, and the picture occasionally went fuzzy or the colors were off.

"What's her real name, anyway?" Gabrielle asked.

Lance shrugged. "No idea," he said. "I'm not even sure whose territory she came from. Some, I guess you would call them species, prefer one region to another. My kind, we're interspersed through all three. I just know she's been here for at least a hundred years."

"How many lives?" Gabrielle looked down.

"Including you? Half a dozen," Lance said. "We think. We know that she has been trading lives sooner rather than later each time. If she wasn't so weirdly fixated on celebrity, she'd pick someone with a lower profile, but she's only grown greedier and more desperate as time goes on."

Like a serial killer, Gabrielle thought. *No, not like. That's what she is. She may not do the dirty work, but the outcome is the same.*

Gabrielle noticed the car slow down again, this time as Lance pulled off the main road to park at a nature overlook. "From here, we walk," he said.

Lance led Gabrielle through a dense forest for what felt like an eternity, shouldering a backpack filled with a first aid kit and water. They did not follow any man-made paths. At least it was still early enough in the season that the woods had yet to fill with thick underbrush. The trees themselves were only beginning to sprout leaves. Yellow and brown leaves crunched underfoot, scaring away chipmunks and squirrels. They chattered to one another from under rocks and high up on tree branches as Lance and Gabrielle intruded upon their home.

"Sorry." Gabrielle apologized to a squirrel, then ducked as an acorn flew at her head.

Lance laughed. "He wants your absence, not your apologies."

Gabrielle's eyes widened. "You can understand him?"

"No, I made an obvious inferential leap, you weirdo." He patted Gabrielle on the back. "I'm not fluent in squirrel."

In their laughter, Gabrielle almost forgot they were not out for a fun hike, even as more sweat trailed down her back. Then Lance put a hand on her arm.

"There," he said, pointing. The forest opened into a clearing. Near the center rose an ancient, misshapen oak tree. From its immense size, Gabrielle knew it must be hundreds of years old. Numerous tumors grew from its thick trunk. Few leaves sprouted from the branches. This tree was not only old—it was dying. She saw a large black hollow at the base of the tree but thought little of it.

Yet.

Instead, Gabrielle was surprised that such a vast meadow felt so pristine and untouched, but as they walked closer to the lone tree at the center, a sense of foreboding crept under her skin. The world darkened. She looked up, expecting to see a cloud moving past the sun, but the sky was clear. She noticed she hadn't heard so much as a single bird or rodent chirp and chatter since they entered the clearing. No flowers grew. Even the grass seemed to point away from the tree, as though straining to escape.

"We go in there to pass through the vortex," Lance said.

Gabrielle's stomach dropped. Of course, he was indicating the hollow in the tree. *Of course.*

"Looks like a tight squeeze," Gabrielle said.

"I think your skinny butt can manage," Lance said, "but if you want to wait for me out here, I'll understand." He said it without malice or judgment. "If anything, I'd rather you did."

"No, I'm going." She tightened her jaw.

Lance removed the backpack and set it on the ground nestled between the base of the tree and a gnarled exposed root. "I don't think we have to worry about anyone taking this," he said.

"Do people avoid places around vortices?" Gabrielle asked.

"Usually," Lance answered. "And any other animals unfortunate enough to pass through never make it back again." He knelt in front of the hollow. "Follow me as close as you can." He climbed through, and by the time only his feet stuck out of the tree, his head should have reached the other side of the trunk. Instead, Gabrielle heard him call, "Coming?"

"Yeah!" she called back as his feet disappeared within. Gabrielle took a deep breath, slipped on her jacket, and knelt on the ground. She ignored the smell of rotting oak and the feel of soft yet sticky cobwebs brushing against her face as she crawled behind him into the dark unknown recesses of the tree.

twenty-three

GABRIELLE WONDERED what happened to any of the spiders responsible for the cobwebs brushing against her face and sticking to her hair as she shimmied through the dark against the cool, damp earth. *Maybe they fit right into Lance's world.* The thought struck her as unfair to the benign creatures, creepy as they were, but she giggled anyway.

Anything to take her mind off what she was doing. She definitely did not want to think of getting stuck somewhere between the tree's hollow and the earth - or worse, in between worlds. Gabrielle took a deep shaky breath as she continued crawling. She could hear Lance moving ahead just fine. So long as he was okay, she was okay. *Right?*

When Lance stopped, her breath caught in her throat. "You may feel a little discombobulated as we pass through the veil between worlds," he said. "The air will be a bit thinner, too. Like reaching the summit of Mount Everest."

Gabrielle did not bother pointing out she'd never climbed Mount Everest, or even left the North American continent, apart from one glaring exception. Instead, she continued forward, trying to steady her breathing. Sure enough, the world went topsy-turvy as she crossed some invisible threshold, like she was in one of those revolving tunnels in a funhouse. Now she felt as though she was climbing up rather than crawling down. Lance's strong arms reached for hers. He helped pull her out of the darkness...

...and into the alien landscape from her dreams. Only it was not some product of her imagination. She had been here before. Gabrielle swooned as she gazed up at the sky, full of unfamiliar constellations and waves of green and magenta light. She knew it from her dreams and memories and from one of Lance's paintings.

"Easy there," Lance said, kneeling beside her.

Gabrielle leaned forward, trying not to retch. Lance lightly rubbed her back, and the feeling passed. "I'm okay now." She rose to her feet, looking around. "I know I wasn't conscious all that long the last time I was here, but it feels different somehow. Quieter."

"I know," Lance said. His expression was grim as he began to walk forward. Gabrielle followed, surveying the barren wasteland of crumbling rocks and burnt tree husks. Some sort of moss grew on the rocks and exposed roots of trees, glowing a toxic shade of yellow green. Vines or something like vines snaked up trees. A small insec-tile creature flew too close to what Gabrielle had mistaken for a leaf. The not-leaf unfurled, then snapped shut on the unsuspecting creature.

A carnivorous plant.

Gabrielle felt unsurprised as she saw other plants resembling sundews and Venus fly traps, even a pitcher plant as big as an actual pitcher. The land was so barren, it only made sense for plants to adapt to the lack of nutrients in the ground. That the cold did not bother them did surprise her, but they seemed to generate their own warmth along with their own light.

"Can you believe this is what passes for summer here?" Lance asked, as though he sensed her thoughts. Maybe he'd just heard Gabrielle sniffling. "There are more hospitable places in this world," he continued, "beautiful, teeming with life, but you'll only find them in underground caverns now. Our ability to thrive without the real light of the sun is waning. Even here, our magic has limits."

"Are we getting close?" Gabrielle asked. Something felt very wrong.

"Just past that thermal pool," Lance said. Gabrielle saw the pool, but she also saw something else. "Oh no," Lance breathed as they walked closer.

In the hazy blue glow that rose from the pool, Gabrielle saw the burnt and bloodied body of a strange creature with mottled brown and green skin, long fangs, and sharp claws on its hands and...just its hands. There were no feet. Black ichor puddled around the torn remains of its midsection. Whether it had clawed at the ground to escape from the pool or to keep from getting pulled in, she could not tell. Beyond the pool, she saw more bodies in varying degrees of ruin. The smell of blood and burnt rotting flesh made her nostrils flare in disgust.

Though Gabrielle recognized these as the vampiric creatures that had fed on her during her time in their world, the violence of their demise horrified her just the same. "What did this to those things?"

"Nothing from our world," Lance said. His wary eyes regarded the thermal pool. "I'm afraid your world isn't the only one to receive unexpected visitors, though they never stay here for long."

"And what's to stop them from..." Gabrielle started to ask, but she remembered they had a more immediate problem. "Oh God, Mason!" Her eyes widened in horror.

Lance knelt beside the remains of the creature. "It's been dead for days, longer than he's been missing. I don't think she left him here." He rose. "We should go."

"But if he's not here, then where is he?"

twenty-four

GABRIELLE FOLLOWED in a cloud of hopelessness as Lance led her back through the vortex and into her own world. The sun had set. Stars began to fill the night sky. And Gabrielle did not notice any of it. She did not even bother to brush the cobwebs out of her hair and clothing, at least until a small spider descended in front of her eyes and she shrieked, swatting away at herself until Lance stopped to help.

"All that you've seen, and you're worried about a little spider?" Lance asked with a gentle smile.

"It startled me. Nobody likes a surprise spider," Gabrielle said. "Not even people who like spiders." She released a heavy sigh as they continued walking. "Lance, what are we going to do?"

"I dunno," he said. "Maybe she still has him in your world somewhere. I have my people watching out for her—disguised as him, obviously. Maybe they've seen something or know where she's staying now, if not his hotel room. I know she checked out of the extended stay hotel she's been living in for the past few weeks."

"You knew where she was this whole time, and you didn't do something sooner?" Gabrielle asked, stopping with her hands on her hips.

"We thought we had more time," Lance said. "Were you that anxious to take over for her in the movie? Sean had me under the impression that acting really wasn't your thing."

"No, it isn't, but..." Gabrielle's eyes widened. "There's still a scene to shoot. She gave me the script pages."

"That's good then, right?" Lance said. "Buys us more time, and maybe you can find something out or provide a distraction when we find wherever she's holed up with Mason."

"Uh, did you forget the part where acting isn't really my thing?" Gabrielle asked. "I passed out in the kindergarten school play. And what if we're too late and she finished him off herself?"

"Then at least we'll know," Lance said, putting his hands on Gabrielle's shoulders and looking into her eyes. "But I have to hope otherwise. And so do you."

Gabrielle looked doubtful. After a moment, she nodded.

Sean looked up when Gabrielle walked into their apartment later that night. He watched as she hung up her winter coat. "You didn't find him?"

"No," Gabrielle said. She removed the sweater she wore over her thermal pajamas and collapsed into the armchair.

Sean's eyes grew wide as Gabrielle told him about her journey with Lance back to his world. "So not only are things from his world coming to our world, things from other worlds are going to his world? What's to stop them from coming here?"

Gabrielle shrugged. "For all we know, they have been. I can't even think about that now. I'm just worried about Mason." She sat up straight. "I know it's the least of my worries, but there's one scene left to film. I have lines to memorize. That I have to speak. On camera."

"Yeah, you're on the schedule to come in for one more fitting tomorrow," Sean said, his tone apologetic. "But I'll be there. For filming, too. We'll get you through this, together."

Gabrielle smiled. "He asked about you," she said after a moment. "Lance. He wanted to know if you were okay. I think you should call him."

Sean shook his head. "We're from two different worlds, Bri," he said. "Literally. It would never work out. I don't even know who or what he really is."

"He's good people," Gabrielle said. "That's what he is."

Sean remained stone-faced as he lay back on the futon with his hands behind his head. Gabrielle knew that look all too well. There would be no reasoning with him tonight.

After a long shower, Gabrielle crawled into bed. Her phone beeped to notify her of a new Tiffany Sharp video, for the ballad she'd heard earlier on the radio. She watched as Tiffany crooned, "If you can't love me for me, just let me be" in a pink stairwell that looked an awful lot like the stairwell of a local bar. She must have filmed it while she was in town for the movie.

Sure enough, Gabrielle recognized the lakeside beach that served as a backdrop for the next scene as Tiffany walked barefoot in the sand wearing, of all things, a long flowing gown with iridescent sequins that shimmered in the moonlight.

Gabrielle fell asleep listening to whatever music the website played next, only to dream of dark places and being dragged by her ankle into a pool of water by an unseen beast. The water turned black with blood.

twenty-five

"I'M BEGINNING to think sleep is vastly overrated," Gabrielle said to Sean the next morning as he handed her a cup of coffee with lots of cream and sugar. She yawned for emphasis as she opened her laptop on the counter to check her email. "Ah, shit."

"What's wrong?" Sean asked.

"A reminder for my meeting with Professor Smith to look at the rough draft of my research paper," Gabrielle said. "Damn it. I never made it past the eighth page. How am I supposed to deal with this on top of everything else?"

"Take what you have, and maybe she'll go easy on you because of the movie. You still have over a month before the final copy is due. And that acting gig will pay more than any academic journal will for your paper," Sean said. "She'll understand. Maybe. Probably not. Worth a try, anyway."

"And that's assuming the checks still get sent to me, and not to *her*," Gabrielle said. "I have to get ready. The meeting's in less than two hours."

. . .

Gabrielle waited outside Professor Smith's office, clutching a folder containing her rough draft – such as it was – to her chest. She forced a smile when the door opened, and the professor ushered her into her office.

Professor Smith was a short but intimidating woman, even in a loose ivory sweater and baggy blue pants. A frizzy mane of long gray hair obscured her aging face. Her steely blue eyes regarded Gabrielle over nondescript eyeglasses.

"I'm having a hard time wrapping things up and going into my conclusion," Gabrielle said. "Work's been keeping me kind of busy." She offered another shaky grin.

"Work keeps me busy, too," Professor Smith said without returning her smile. "I still have deadlines to meet." Her tone was stern but matter-of-fact. "Let's see what you have." She accepted the papers from Gabrielle's outstretched hands and began to read. After she read the last page, she leaned back in her chair.

Gabrielle tried not to fidget as she waited for her to speak.

After a few moments, Professor Smith leaned forward. She gathered up Gabrielle's papers with her weathered hands and gave them to her. "You don't have anywhere near enough, but what you have so far isn't bad," she said. "Something to consider is what the phrase 'strong female character' means to you in particular."

"Well, Hollywood interprets it as replacing a typical male lead with a woman and giving her lots of weapons, but what viewers really want are fully developed characters that aren't purely good or bad. Characters who reflect the full range of human experience," Gabrielle said.

"Yes, I see you mention that in your rough draft, but it's hardly a new insight, and it doesn't help me understand why this topic is important to you," Professor Smith said. "I guess what I'm looking for is an explanation of strength. Is there only brute force, or can a character demonstrate strength in other ways?"

Gabrielle began to answer, but Professor Smith continued.

"Don't say anything now. I just want you to think about it as you finish your rough draft. Consider movie characters that subvert the usual tropes and demonstrate strength in ways we take for granted."

"Okay," Gabrielle said, sliding the papers back into her folder. "Thank you, Professor Smith. You gave me a lot to consider."

"I'll see you next month," Professor Smith said. "I expect you to be better prepared."

"Yes," Gabrielle said as she rose to leave. "Absolutely."

Gabrielle sat in front of her laptop, staring at her research paper. She knew Professor Smith wanted her to think about movie characters that showed strength in other ways, but instead she found herself thinking about the women she knew in real life.

Desiree was only a freshman, but she had all the self-assurance Gabrielle lacked. Even Chase never got under her skin, not really. And nobody would bat an eye if she said she wanted to direct.

Monica, well, she was a bit of a hot mess, "hot" being the operative word, but she was not afraid to speak her mind. Gabrielle had to admit she admired that about Monica even more than her perfect hair and enviable figure.

And then there were Natalia and Tiffany. Gabrielle remembered how Natalia's commanding presence filled the room. She had all of Desiree's confidence and Monica's directness, albeit tempered with greater tact. And Tiffany made a point of being in control even as she kept things fun and light.

Gabrielle wished she had even half their confidence. Maybe if she did, she would know how to rescue Mason. Maybe he would not even need rescuing. And maybe, just maybe, she was the wrong person to write about strength in the first place.

. . .

Sean was already working when Gabrielle drove to a large warehouse where the indoor prom scenes were being filmed. The largest room was cordoned into two sections. Gabrielle glanced at the section decorated for the prom with gold, silver, and purple streamers and balloons. Across the way, Natalia stood talking to Harlow Hanson. Looking beautiful in a strapless pink satin dress, her lustrous brown hair falling in loose curls, she gave a little wave when she saw Gabrielle,

Not-Mason stood nearby and gave Gabrielle a mocking wave of his own. She ignored him and continued walking past the next section, where extras in formal attire sat in chairs or milled around the craft service table. Someone bumped into her.

"Oh, God, not you again," Gabrielle said as she glared down at the old man in an outdated tuxedo. Her dear old friend Mickey McDeathBreath grinned up at her, unfazed, as she asked, "Do you own this building, too?"

"No." Mickey laughed, but it sounded more like a wheeze. "I guess you and I both got the acting bug after that last movie. I'm playing a chaperone, but I told them I'd be more than happy to stand in for the lead actor if it meant I had a chance to share the screen with you."

Gabrielle caught his wrist before he could touch her bottom. "If I find out that you've laid a hand on any of my extras, I'll break it," she told him.

"Yes, ma'am." Mickey looked at her like the world's saddest most wrinkly puppy dog before he retreated to the craft service table.

Desiree walked up to Gabrielle, wearing a headset and holding several water bottles. "Wow." She almost sounded impressed. "That man's either going to have you fired or ask you to marry him. Bad day?"

"To say the least," Gabrielle replied, running a hand through her unruly curls.

"Your boy's been having a rough day himself," Desiree said. She winced as she listened to someone bark orders on the headset. "The director is not happy with today's footage, which means Harlow isn't happy, and neither is Chase. Hope Mason gets it together before your big scene on Thursday." She turned to go. "Wardrobe is in the last office on the right," she called over her shoulder.

Gabrielle walked down to the room Desiree indicated. Sean smiled and handed her one hanger with a dress and another with a strapless bra. "You can try it on behind that curtain," he said.

"Are you sure I can fill it out?" Gabrielle looked skeptical as she accepted the hangers.

"I already swapped the bra for the right size," Sean said with a smirk. "And I warned Hilary you may need some extra pinning. All that running around with Mason, you've hardly found time to eat."

"Well, I did work up a sweat yesterday," Gabrielle said as she undressed in the makeshift changing room. "Just not in the fun sexy way," she muttered, stepping into the velvety dress. Its peacock blue color reminded her of her car, but she would never pick something so vibrant to wear. The dress hugged her body until it flared at the knee. The slit came up to her thigh. But the sweetheart neckline and off-shoulder sleeves worried her more.

"Need help with the zipper?" Sean asked.

Gabrielle reluctantly stepped out from behind the curtain. "I'm not sure I can pull this off," she said.

"I don't think you'll be lacking volunteers to help you out," Sean said as he carefully zipped up the dress. "Wow. Would you look at that." He turned Gabrielle to face a full-length mirror, then took a few steps back to admire her himself. "You know, I don't think I've ever seen you in a dress before. The fit is perfect."

Gabrielle gazed at her reflection. The dress did look spectacular, and it felt better than she expected the way it hugged her curves, but she felt self-conscious all the same with her frizzy curls and bare face. "It's my clavicle that sells the look, isn't it?"

Sean laughed. "I mean, the décolletage is nice, too, if you're into that sort of thing."

"It would have looked better on me," said a voice from the doorway. "I need a clean shirt." Not-Mason walked up to a rack of dress shirts, removing his jacket and tossing it over a chair. "Maria throws her drink on me in this scene. They were hoping to get the shot in one take. Unfortunately, her performance was lacking."

"She's not the one having performance issues, from what I've heard," Gabrielle said, turning to smirk at Sean as Not-Mason began to change his shirt.

Sean raised his eyebrows in warning.

"You're never going to find him, you know," Not-Mason said as he finished buttoning his shirt. He slipped his jacket on and walked behind Gabrielle. "But we can always pretend he never left. That's what actors do." He leaned in close to whisper in her ear. "I think you'll find I'm not having any issues with my performance." His reflection wavered in the mirror, like a distorted image with a blueish tint on an old television set.

"Are you sure about that?" Gabrielle watched his reflection with interest. "I'm told it's harder to maintain an illusion in our world than it is in yours. It gets even harder the more you have to alter your appearance." She grinned. "Every now and then, I can almost see you as you really are. Even Natalia would have been a tough sale—she's so little—but Mason? That must be exhausting."

Not-Mason's jaw stiffened. He left the room without another word.

"Damn, Bri," Sean said. "I know you're angry, but if everything you've told me is true, she might target someone else, even if they have less celebrity than Mason or Natalia."

"And I'm still no closer to finding Mason." Gabrielle sighed and stepped behind the curtain to change. As she was pulling her jeans back on, her phone buzzed, and she slid it out of her back pocket. "It's Lance," she said. "They found out where she's staying. I have to go. How many hours of filming do they have left?"

Sean shrugged. "A few scenes. It depends on how many takes they need to get the shots they want. I'm here until the bitter end, so I can warn you."

"Thank you!" Gabrielle kissed him on the cheek.

"Be safe!" Sean called after her.

"Always."

twenty-six

GABRIELLE PARKED in front of Lance's home. He opened the door before she could knock. "The agents have been watching the place since they tracked her down," he said as they walked back down the driveway to his car. "We generally don't involve humans, but these are unique circumstances."

"You're not going to work some sort of mojo to wipe our memories when all this is over, are you?" Gabrielle climbed into the passenger side of the car.

Lance did not answer until he started to drive. "With everything that you've seen and experienced these past few weeks, I'm not sure I can do that without causing brain damage."

Gabrielle noticed that he did not rule out the capability. There were still so many things she did not know about Lance or beings from his world, let alone other beings from other worlds. "Whatever killed those creatures on your world, can it get into ours?"

"For all we know, it already has," Lance said. "Like I said, those visitors don't stick around for long, and I don't know if anything from their world possesses the same level of intelligence as we do. They're curious and destructive, and that may be the extent of it."

"Or maybe that information is above your pay grade, too,"

Gabrielle observed, her frown deepening. "Knowing there's monsters that can kill other monsters, and they both have a way to visit our world, is not a very comforting thought."

"Look at it this way," Lance said. "You've gone your entire life thinking your world was a certain way. Will knowing it isn't as you thought change how you live? It's like people swimming in the ocean. They don't see what a pilot flying above them sees. As far as they know, they're safe. And the vast majority of the time, they are."

"Except a lot of people do avoid the ocean," Gabrielle said.

"But are their lives any better for it?" Lance asked. "It's always going to be something. Odds are, it won't be a shark attack, even if you swim all the time. And despite sharks being endangered, there's still more of them than anything from out of this world. There's no reason you can't live a perfectly normal life after we find Mason." He smiled at her. "As normal as life in Hollyweird can be, anyway."

"I guess I just want to know if I should worry about some big alien invasion before I get too caught up in bills and 401k plans," Gabrielle said. "That's all."

"Look, even I have to pay the bills," Lance said, laughing.

Lance drove to an abandoned building near the shore of Lake Erie. He pulled the car into an alleyway. "Just a minute," he said after they climbed out of the car. Gabrielle watched as Lance closed his eyes in concentration. Then she gasped. His car could no longer be seen.

"Just in case," Lance said. "Hopefully we'll be long gone before she gets back. And she doesn't try to park in the same spot," he added. "The other agents can handle the rest."

"Is it just the two of them?" Gabrielle asked.

"Two more came from another region," Lance said, "but two should be sufficient. We don't want to take any more chances. Are you ready to go in?"

Gabrielle stared at the crumbling brick building. "I remember reading that this place is condemned, but the city is going back and forth with some historical society. I can't believe she chose this place of all places to stay."

"She didn't. She's been staying in Mason's room at the hotel," Lance said. "She just comes here a couple times a day to check on him."

Gabrielle hated the thought of Mason being held hostage in an ancient decrepit building that looked like it would collapse in on itself at any moment. Meanwhile, his double was staying across the hall from the original target.

"Why didn't the agents save Mason themselves?"

"A familiar face seemed best," Lance said, pulling a flashlight out of his pocket and handing it to Gabrielle. "He's going to have too many questions as it is." He pushed on a door. It opened with a noisy creak. "After you."

The sun had only just set, but the stairwell was dark. It smelled of dank mildew and decay. Gabrielle turned on her flashlight. "What floor?"

"Second, but watch the third step," Lance said.

Gabrielle took a couple of steps. They were concrete, but a large chunk was missing from the third, so she skipped it and used the rail to pull herself up to the fourth. She could barely hear over the sound of her heart beating in her ears. By the time she reached the second floor, she felt shaky and out of breath. She coughed into her elbow.

"The air's pretty foul in here, isn't it?" Lance asked, keeping his voice low.

"I don't even want to think of how many health codes this building violates," Gabrielle whispered. She coughed again. "Poor Mason. He's been trapped in this hellhole for what...three days now?"

"Third room on your left," Lance said. "Someone is downstairs watching out for her, and the other three are close by in case we run into any unexpected problems."

"You don't have walkie talkies. How do you know where...?"

Gabrielle paused mid-sentence. "You don't need walkie talkies, do you? What, do you share some sort of telepathic link?"

Lance nodded. "I can also read thoughts and plant suggestions," he said, "but I've never invaded your privacy, and everything you've done, you chose to do. Your move." He indicated the door with a nod.

Gabrielle pressed her lips together. Then she walked to the door and pushed it open. An insect skittered past her foot. Light barely penetrated the boarded-up windows. She forced herself to step into the room, shining her flashlight on the floor until she saw the soles of someone's shoes.

"Mason? Mason!"

Gabrielle raced toward the figure sitting in the corner of the room. The scream that followed was ear-shattering.

twenty-seven

"STAY the hell away from me, you crazy bitch!"

Gabrielle stopped in her tracks. Mason struggled to push himself away from her with his feet, but his back was flush against the wall, his arms bound behind his back. When she shone her flashlight on his face, he appeared almost crazed with anger. She kneeled on the floor. "Mason, it's me. It's not...her."

"Who? Your sister?" Mason asked. "Do you *even* have a sister?" The anger in his eyes gave way to hurt and confusion.

"No," Gabrielle said, trying to placate him, "and I can explain, but we need to get you out of here before she gets back."

"Don't you mean *him*?" Mason asked, scowling. "Or more to the point, *me*? Before *I* get back?"

"Not really the time to be pedantic, Mason. We gotta go." Mason cringed at her touch but allowed her to begin untying the rope that bound his wrists.

Not to intrude, but the other Mason is coming.

Not cool, Dude, Gabrielle thought back, even though she knew the alternative mode of communication was unavoidable under their present circumstances. She worked harder at untying the rope.

Gabrielle's ears pricked at the sound of footsteps on the stairwell.

There came the sound of a scuffle in the hallway, then not-Mason burst through the door. Lance stumbled in after him, pressing his hand against a bleeding gash in his forehead. "Bri, look out!"

Not-Mason charged at Gabrielle, raising a deadly sharp dagger over his head, coated with green dripping ooze. *Poison?* The strange iridescent metal of the blade suggested otherworldly origins. Gabrielle froze, mesmerized, when a woman with dark brown skin dropped from a hole in the ceiling. The knife skittered across the floor as a pale man with a mustache ran in to retrieve the knife. Both wore nondescript black suits. A third agent with a blond buzz cut strode in next to help the woman lift not-Mason, no, not Mason at all anymore, to her feet.

Now Gabrielle saw her as she really was: the strange translucent skin, long raven black hair, and angry eyes that failed to settle on a color, instead flashing from blue to green, even amber like Lance's. "You can't make me go back there," she snarled. "They'll find me."

"We already have found you," Lance said, sitting on the ground. A fourth agent had entered the room. She tended to his wound. Somehow, he maintained his human appearance despite his injury.

The defeated being on the floor threw her head back and laughed maniacally. "You have no idea what's coming." Her laughter turned to sobs as she cried out. "All I had to do was find a safe place to hide it, and she would reward me with the life of my dreams. I was stupid, so stupid. If she was so powerful, I wouldn't need to hide. But then, she never would have needed my help at all."

"Who is *she*?" Lance pressed.

The being shook her head. She was done talking.

"She's talking about those things, isn't she?" Gabrielle asked. "The ones that *visited* your home?" She did not want to go into greater detail with Mason standing there. He looked shell-shocked as it was.

"I dunno," Lance said. "Maybe. Doesn't matter. Your role in this is over, that much I can assure you." He turned to acknowledge

Mason. "We should get you home. My *associates* will take care of her."

Lance drove Gabrielle and Mason back to his home first. "We can't take you back to the hotel looking like this," Gabrielle explained. "It would lead to too many questions. Especially if there's any paparazzi lurking about."

"I have a few questions myself," Mason said, but to Lance.

"Are you sure you want answers?" Lance asked.

Mason shook his head. "You know what, I probably don't." He looked at Gabrielle for the first time since they left the abandoned building. "I just want to crawl into bed and forget the last few weeks even happened."

Lance found Mason a clean pair of clothes to change into while he showered. They were about the same height, so the fit was good.

"Ready to go?" Lance asked. He opened the front door.

Mason walked past him to go outside. Gabrielle followed. He turned to her. "Isn't that your car parked in front?"

Gabrielle nodded, furrowing her brow in confusion.

"Then you don't need a ride from him." Mason said. Gabrielle was taken aback by the harshness in his voice. "I don't want you anywhere near me."

Then I've got some bad news about tomorrow. Gabrielle blinked back tears.

Lance squeezed her shoulder as he walked by. *Give him time.*

Really? Gabrielle stared at him, lifting a hand.

Sorry.

twenty-eight

"DID you know Lance can read minds?" Gabrielle asked the next day as Sean drove to the park. Tonight, she had to shoot a scene with Mason in a garden of cherry blossom trees. It was not the last scene of the movie, but it was the last scene they had to film because they had to wait for the cherry blossoms to bloom.

"Until a few days ago, I thought Lance was a normal guy," Sean said. "He reads minds?"

"He can talk in them, too," Gabrielle said, staring out the window. "It's a little unnerving."

"Sounds intrusive." Sean scowled.

"He promised that he never invaded my privacy. I'm sure that's true for you, too," she added quickly. "Still, it seems like there could be some practical applications of such talents in a relationship. With consent, of course."

"It's over, Bri." Sean sighed. He pulled the car into a parking space. From there, they could see the lights and cameras being set up in the garden. "I'll see you in a bit," Sean said as he walked to the trailer being used by the wardrobe department.

"Hair and makeup are right in the next trailer," Desiree said as she walked by.

Gabrielle almost bumped into Mason as he walked down the steps of the trailer. "Hey," she said. "How are you?"

Mason did not answer. He barely even glanced at Gabrielle as he brushed past.

"Oof," Monica said to Gabrielle. "That was cold."

"It's called tact, Monica," said Drew Gibson. The electric-blue-haired makeup artist rolled their eyes. "You're almost as bad as Jenna." They swept blush across Natalia's dimpled cheeks.

The actress's kind brown eyes met Gabrielle's in the mirror. "Did something happen after the party last weekend? Is that why you didn't want to hang out on Sunday?"

Gabrielle shook her head as she sat down in front of Monica.

"Something must have happened," Natalia pressed. "He's been acting weird all week. Then he wanted to hang out the other night. But, I dunno, his vibe was off."

"Yeah, he hasn't really been himself." Gabrielle shrugged. "Filming is about to wrap. Maybe he didn't know how to break things off."

"Well, I'll be giving him a piece of mind when we get back to the hotel," Natalia said. She looked like she wanted to say more but waited while Drew applied lipstick. "I promised Tiffany I'd look out for you." She winked at Gabrielle's reflection in the mirror.

"Thanks," Gabrielle said, "but it's not really his fault. Sometimes things just aren't meant to be." She stared into space as Monica applied mousse and began to curl her hair.

"You're all set," Drew told Natalia. "Final – final – looks," they said as they snapped a photo with their smartphone. Natalia gave Gabrielle one last smile as she left the trailer.

"I know we've never exactly been close," Monica said, "but if you need someone to talk to, I'm here for you. And I won't say anything to anybody else because I'm not actually like Jenna at all." She glared at Drew, who smiled back, unfazed.

"It's funny," Gabrielle said. "I never actually went to prom."

"Really?" Gabrielle braced herself for a snarky remark, but

instead Monica said, "To be honest, you probably didn't miss out on much. It's kind of overrated. You spend all this money on the tickets and the dress, and all you have to show for it are embarrassing pictures with someone you'd never consider dating in college. Now walking the red carpet or going to an award show, that will be amazing."

"I had a blast at my prom," Drew said. "Danced the whole-"

"Drew, read the room," Monica said, exasperated.

Monica and Drew continued debating the value of school dances while doing Gabrielle's hair and makeup. She just stared down at her rumpled tear-stained script, hoping to get this nightmare over with as soon as possible. She would almost rather confront any number of alien invaders than face Mason again. On camera, no less.

"How're you holding up?" Sean asked as he zipped Gabrielle into her dress.

"It's my script," she muttered.

"That good, huh?" Sean gave her a sympathetic look as he fastened a delicate gold chain around her neck, from which hung a single aquamarine pendant. She put on the matching earrings herself, though she barely looked at her reflection. If she had, she would have noticed the delicate finger waves framing a face that appeared naturally flushed, full berry-stained lips, and pretty if sad blue eyes framed by dark lashes.

"Don't suppose I can coax a smile out of you before I take your picture?" Sean asked.

"Does it matter?" Gabrielle asked. "If we don't finish filming tonight, I'll throw myself off the Peace Bridge or something."

"Okay, now you're just being dramatic," Sean said, raising an eyebrow.

"I'm supposed to be dramatic," Gabrielle said as she slipped on her shoes. "I'm an actress! For tonight, anyway." She gave him a rueful smile as he took a couple of pictures.

"I'm saving these," he said. "My little girl's all grown up."

"Shut up." Gabrielle rolled her eyes.

"Break a leg," Sean said as he opened the trailer door for her. "Ideally Chase's if you can find him!"

Mason was already on set when Gabrielle left the wardrobe trailer, finishing a scene with Natalia. Her heart caught in her throat at the sight of him in his tuxedo. He glanced in her direction, and his jaw tightened.

Gabrielle prayed for a vortex to open beneath her as she approached.

I can do this, she told herself.

Can I, though?

twenty-nine

GABRIELLE COULD ONLY HOPE the boom mic did not pick up the loud thumping of her heartbeat during sound check. She stared at the ground, the cherry blossoms, the sky--anything to avoid eye contact with Mason until she had no choice but to look at him.

Everything about the setting yelled "romance," from the bright stars set against the velvety black sky to the natural perfume of the delicate pink petals and the feel of a gentle breeze. The picture-perfect setting.

"Rolling," Chase called.

"Scene ninety-three, take one," Desiree said in front of the camera. She clapped the sticks and moved out of frame.

"And action," Harlan called.

Gabrielle looked at Mason. The script called for tears. She did not have to fake it as she said, "I really am sorry for everything I've done," she said. "I never meant to hurt anyone, I swear." She tried to touch Mason's arm, but he pulled away. His jaw tightened. Though the exchange was written in the script, it still stung.

"It doesn't matter what your intentions were, Victoria. It's wrong to deceive people." Mason glared, his green eyes ferocious. "And you hurt someone I care about a lot. You're not that someone. You never will be."

He turned and walked away, leaving Gabrielle to stand with tears streaming down her face. She did not wipe them away. It was not in the script. She just watched him go.

"Cut!" Harlan said. He strode toward Gabrielle. "That was a perfect take!" He patted Gabrielle on the back. "You really brought a fresh vulnerability to the character tonight. To be honest, I didn't know you had it in you."

Gabrielle gave him a wan smile. "Thanks."

"Take five while we reset for Zack's close-ups. Maintain that same level of performance, and we should breeze right through the rest of tonight's filming," Harlow said.

Gabrielle blinked away the last of her tears as she walked to a chair that had been set up for her a short distance from where they were filming. She felt grateful Mason's chair was several yards away. Desiree gave her a sympathetic look as she handed her a bottle of water. "How are you doing?" she asked.

"I'm managing," Gabrielle said. "It's the longest I've..." She trailed off. She was about to say it was the longest she'd ever had to speak in public, and the first on camera—but as far as Desiree or anyone else knew, she had been playing the role of Victoria all along. "It's the longest I've been around him since..."

"Things went kerflooey?" Desiree said.

"Something like that." Gabrielle took a drink of her water. Drew and Monica came over to touch up her hair and makeup. She saw Mason standing near his chair out of the corner of her eye. Though she sensed him looking in her direction, she pretended not to notice. She just wanted to get through filming, go home, and go to bed.

Several takes later, including close-ups of "Zack" and "Victoria" and a few wide shots, Harlow finally yelled, "Cut!" Gabrielle had never felt so drained, not even when she had literally been left drained and bloody in the woods. She had a newfound appreciation for actors. Even without the added emotional turmoil of her circumstances, she knew she would have been exhausted by the end of tonight's filming.

Gabrielle did not even remember if she smiled to acknowledge the applause when Harlow called a wrap on her character, nor did she notice a crack of lightning or distant roll of thunder. She just returned to the tent in a daze.

* * *

As Gabrielle walked to the parking lot to wait for Sean in his car, she was startled by a large group of reporters and camera crews rushing toward her.

"Bri, is it true you were only using Mason Wright to raise your profile?" One reporter pushed in front of the others to shove a microphone in Gabrielle's face.

A flashbulb fired.

Gabrielle blinked. She shook herself as she regrouped. "I never wanted to be an actress," she replied truthfully. "I just really like Mason. But I also understand if he doesn't want to see me again after...after everything that's happened." She shrugged as she gazed at the reporters and photographers in front of her.

Several more muscled their way forward and held out their microphones. Gabrielle backed away, holding up her hands.

"I'm done talking now."

Nobody moved, but another flashbulb fired. Gabrielle raised an eyebrow in irritation.

"So, you can like, go, or whatever."

Sean pushed through the crowd. He placed a protective hand on Gabrielle's shoulder and squeezed. "You heard the woman. Go." Not until a bolt of lightning lit the sky and heavy drops of rain began to fall did the crowd disperse.

"Seriously?"

Gabrielle gave Sean a grateful smile as he held his jacket open over her head to guide her away from the flashing lights and shouting reporters. She glanced back over her shoulder, pursing her lips. "I'd almost rather take my chances with those awful blood-sucking monsters again than face any more tabloid reporters," she confessed.

Sean laughed. "Is there a difference?" He wrapped an arm around her shoulder. "Let's get you home. It's all over now."

Gabrielle leaned against Sean on the couch in a t-shirt and flannel pajama shorts, her hair still damp and a blanket wrapped around her shoulders. They ate popcorn while watching her embarrassing encounter with all those reporters and photographers on the evening news.

"I still can't believe this is my life."

Wide-eyed, Gabrielle stared at her bewildered face on the television screen. She once again felt grateful that Monica and Drew had done such an amazing job on her hair and makeup. She looked sad and tired, but at least her mascara stayed put.

"Yeah, it's the paparazzi hounding you." Sean snorted. "*That's* what takes the insanity of your life to the next level."

Gabrielle giggled.

"You really did an amazing job today," Sean said, reaching for the remote to turn off the television set. "Not just with those reporters, but the movie scene, too. I'm proud of you. Are you sure you don't want to act?"

"Oh God, no," Gabrielle said. "I really don't know how people like Mason and Natalia do it day in and day out. Having to say those same lines over and over again...I swear, if Harlow requested one more take for safety, I was going to scream. And you know what," Gabrielle continued, "I didn't realize how short Mason was until I had to remove my heels for most of the shots. So annoying. He flubbed his lines once, too."

"Is this denial?" Sean asked. "I think this is denial. It sounds a little too petty to be acceptance."

Gabrielle ignored him.

"So, what's next?" Sean asked.

"Well, Desiree did ask me if I was going to be a PA for this indie film coming to town in a couple weeks," Gabrielle said.

"Oh," Sean said. "Fun."

"I put in an application to be second AD instead." A grin spread across Gabrielle's face.

"Really?" Sean returned her smile.

"I know, right?" Gabrielle said. "I guess after everything that's happened to you and I, the film industry doesn't seem so intimidating anymore. Mason, Natalia, Harlow—they're all just regular people, right?"

Sean nodded.

Gabrielle gave him a pointed look. "Life is way too short to worry about taking chances."

"Mmm." Sean smirked. "I'm glad it only took having your life hijacked by some homicidal alien fairy to figure it out."

Gabrielle playfully nudged his shoulder with her own.

Her phone rang.

"Mom, hey..."

"I saw the news," Mrs. Johnson said. "Are you okay?"

"I'm fine, Mom, just really tired." Gabrielle rolled her eyes at Sean. He raised an eyebrow. She nodded at him, taking a deep breath. "Look, I've been thinking about what you said, but I think the best thing for my career is to stay in school here. Another movie is coming to town, and I applied to be second AD. I think I have a real shot."

"I think you do, too," her mother said. "All I ever wanted was for you to apply yourself. It's not the career path I envisioned, but seeing you on TV tonight, it looks like you have a handle on things. You were very...poised."

"Thanks, Mom."

"I always tell you to be safe," Mrs. Johnson said, "but maybe that's the wrong approach."

"I'll be smart," Gabrielle said. "G'night, Mom."

thirty

"SO HOW MANY more times are you going to play that same Tiffany Sharp song on repeat?" Sean asked through Gabrielle's door the following morning. "I can hear the crying. It's starting to bum me out."

Gabrielle paused the music on her laptop. She opened the door to glare at Sean. "I've been through a lot, okay? You grieve in your annoying quiet way and leave me to grieve noisily in mine." She reached for a tissue to blow her nose before dropping it into the nearly full wastebasket by her door.

"Well, do you think you can take a break for a minute? Wash your raccoon eyes, do something about your hair?" Sean used his hand to indicate the wildness. "You have a visitor."

"Your *face* has a visitor," Gabrielle pushed her door shut.

"What?!"

"Just give me a minute." Gabrielle ran a comb through her wild curls and reached for what felt like the hundredth facial wipe since last night. She was beginning to think that her mascara was never coming off. Tearproof, rainproof, even makeup-remover-proof.

Once she was satisfied with her appearance, Gabrielle slipped a hoodie over her tank top and exchanged her pajama shorts for running shorts. She opened her door.

Sean looked at her with the hint of a smile. "I'll be in my room."

Gabrielle furrowed her brow as she stepped into the hall. Sean gave her a quick hug before he walked to his room and shut the door. Gabrielle walked into the living room. Her eyes widened. Mason looked up. They stared at each other until she gave a weak gesture in the direction of the futon. "Would you like to sit down?"

"Yeah, right," Mason said. "Sitting's good."

Gabrielle was not the only performer Drew had worked their magic on yesterday. Without makeup, Mason not only appeared paler, but he still had shadows under his eyes from his ordeal with the doppelgänger. Despite that, he was still the most handsome man Gabrielle had seen. Her heart leapt into her throat as she sat across from him in the armchair.

After an awkward silence, they both tried to speak. "I'm sorry," Mason began as Gabrielle said, "I think you owe me an apology."

"Wait, what?" Mason asked, bewildered.

Gabrielle realized Mason *was* apologizing. For a moment, she wished she could take back her own words, but for some crazy reason she decided to plow ahead anyway. "I don't think it's fair to blame me for something that began when I was the one poisoned and unconscious in another world entirely, and I don't know how I could have possibly told you the truth without you thinking I was crazy." Mason rose from the futon, but Gabrielle only spit the words out faster. "Besides, you only liked me because I looked like her, but I wasn't as aggressive, and you wanted to feel like you were the one in con-"

Mason kneeled in front of Gabrielle. He placed his hands on either side of her face and started to kiss her.

"...trol," Gabrielle finished. "Just like you're trying to be in control now." She crossed her arms and scowled.

Mason sat right there on the floor and looked up at her, sheepish and confused. After a moment, he said, "Actually, that was me giving up control, though I suppose I can see how it might look different from your perspective. I don't actually know what I'm doing." He shrugged. "I just wanted to kiss you, so I kissed you."

"Yeah, well, read the room," Gabrielle said, though she was at a loss herself. Sean released an audible groan of exasperation from his bedroom.

Mason pushed himself off the floor and sat across from Gabrielle on the futon once more. "Getting a better read on the other room, if I'm being quite honest," he said.

Gabrielle bit her lip on a smile. "Yeah, well, Sean knows a thing or two about relationships built on lies," she said. "They have a way of falling apart."

"Maybe," Mason said, "but it's like you said - had you told me the truth, I may not have believed you. And maybe you're right about me being drawn to you for all the wrong reasons, but the attraction felt mutual. Given the extreme circumstances, I'd like to give it another go."

He gave Gabrielle a lopsided grin that made her melt, but she found herself saying, "I'll think about it."

His smile faded.

"You called me a bitch," she reminded him.

"I called *her* a bitch. She poisoned me, tied me up, and left me in an abandoned building. Then she had the nerve to steal my face, and now I find myself wondering how accurate the rest was." Gabrielle struggled to maintain a straight face as he continued. "Mostly I just feel gutted that I hurt your feelings." Mason reached for her hand.

"It's okay," Gabrielle said, squeezing his hand in return. "It was an extreme circumstance, like you said."

"The wrap party is tomorrow night," Mason said. "They're renting the rooftop lounge at my hotel. I'd love to go together, no matter what you decide." He tucked a strand of hair behind her ears, gazing into her eyes.

"I'll text you," was all she could say

. . .

"Are you freaking kidding me?" Sean asked after Mason left the apartment. He sat down on the futon, his face incredulous as he stared at Gabrielle.

She gave him an innocent smile before typing something on her phone. "We're from two different worlds, Sean. How could it possibly work out? Sooner or later, he'll get bored, or I'll get lonely. Nothing is meant to last forever."

"You're twenty-one years old, Bri. It doesn't need to last forever!" Sean ran his hands through his hair.

"That's true," Gabrielle said. "For all anyone knows, the world could end tomorrow. It's like I said last night. Life's too short not to take a chance. I'd rather try and see what happens than spend the rest of my life wondering what could have been."

Sean narrowed his eyes. "You're not just talking about you and Mason, anymore, are you?"

Gabrielle's grin widened. "Nope."

"It's not the same, Bri. When I say we're from two different worlds, it's a literal truth."

Gabrielle shrugged. "Still closer than New Zealand."

"They did say I could bring a plus one for the party tomorrow," Sean said. "Double date?"

"I already sent the text."

Gabrielle joined Sean on the futon, kissing his cheek before laying her head on his shoulder. She did not know what tomorrow or the next day had in store for them, but for the first time in a long time, she did not feel afraid.

epilogue

LANCE LOOKED DOWN at the message from Sean with a bittersweet smile. Gabrielle's story was once again her own to complete. Lance did not know if there was a place for him in Sean's. But maybe he didn't have to decide just yet. He was about to accept the invitation to a party when someone knocked on the door.

A tall man with a blond buzz cut walked in and sat on the arm of the couch. He didn't bother removing his sunglasses. "Still haven't found out who sent her here or what she left behind," he said.

"What's my directive?"

The agent shrugged. "Continue monitoring known entities. Be on the lookout for anything strange."

"Do we think it's connected to what I observed back home?"

"It's possible." The agent rose. "I have a suspected breach to investigate in New York City, but it appears unrelated." He frowned. "I'd never say so to the higher-ups, but I'm worried about the sustainability of the program."

"Indeed," Lance said as he opened the door.

The agent walked past him outside, but turned back. He lowered his sunglasses. "The number of people who know of our existence is growing. The Lady wants our assurance it won't grow any further. And you know how she feels about letting anyone get too close."

Lance nodded, then closed the door.

Made in the USA
Las Vegas, NV
02 June 2022

49687408R00105